FAIRY TALES

M. A. Valdellon

Published by M. A. Valdellon
www.melissavaldellon.com

Cover design by Elena Lavrova

ISBN-13: 978-0692065235
ISBN-10: 0692065237

If I'm honest, I have to tell you I still read fairy tales and I like them best of all.

- Audrey Hepburn

CONTENTS

1 | Before Midnight

June 1999

"All right. You can open your eyes now."

Megan Lee did as she was told and looked out her window. Her mouth dropped open slightly and her breath caught in her throat for a moment. Then the shock was gone and her mouth curved up into a bright smile to match the twinkling that had come into her eyes. She sat back amazed as her companion went out and around to open the door for her. Her gloved hand took his offered one and she stepped out of the limo.

She felt like she was in a dream world. Here she was, her petite frame dressed as a princess for the night in a slim, silvery dinner gown, a black shawl draped around her shoulders. Most of her long black hair had been pinned up, leaving wisps of some of her shorter hair framing her face. The only jewelry she wore was the necklace her family had given her earlier that day. On a thin golden chain hung a delicate golden rose. "It's your month's flower," her sister had reminded her. "The most beautiful flower in the world for one of the most beautiful women I know," her dad had smiled, giving her a warm, fatherly embrace. "It suits you," her mom had kidded. "The thorns represent the hardships that life will bring on the way to

1

something beautiful and worth all the trouble. Then, there's the idea that you put up barriers for yourself so that people have to work to get to know you, but for those who know you best, they can recognize the beauty found within."

"People are staring," she found herself speaking low to her friend.

"And why shouldn't they be staring? You're easily the most beautiful person here tonight. I consider myself to be a very lucky man to be here with you."

"Ken, are you flirting with me again?" She turned to the man beside her and grinned.

"Of course not. I'm merely complimenting you. There's a difference. Now, if I was flirting with you, I know I'd get in trouble with my girlfriend because I know you'll let her know everything that happens tonight."

She laughed. "You mean what she hasn't seen between us since we left after dinner."

"She was there during dinner?" He put on an innocent face. "I didn't even notice. I couldn't take my eyes off you for a moment."

"Flirt," she smiled.

"One of the best," he smiled back.

"And oh so humble," she laughed.

"Hey now, you should know better than talk about me like that."

"Oh, that's right. No need to state the obvious since we've established the fact that someone's got a superiority complex."

"Only when it comes to the world of flirting and relationships, as you call it. We both know you're far superior to me everywhere else."

"Oh really?"

"What? Has it become a crime for me to say nice things about you now?"

"No…" she started to say.

"I get it," he laughed, stopping her effectively before she could say anymore. "Seriously though. It's your big day. I should think you're used to hearing nice things about you by now, especially tonight."

"Now that's something I doubt I'll ever get used to."

"Doubt now, but I'll bet anything I have that you will be proved wrong on that one someday."

"Again, are we back to being that sure of ourselves?"

"Only because this time, I know I'm right. Once you find that certain someone in your life who you're meant to be with until the end of time, I will be right there saying 'I told you so'."

"Please. That kind of stuff only happens in fairy tales, never to people like me."

"Oh, I don't know. I think we're all up for one fairy tale or another at some point in our lives."

"And this is coming from someone who once said that fairy tales were silly fantasies. Didn't you say that two years ago when we still lived next door to each other at the dorms?"

"I did, and I take my words back. Life can be a fairy tale come true if you let it."

"How enchanting," she laughed. "I'll let your girlfriend know how much of a romantic you've become. I'm sure she'll be glad to know that she's changed you so much."

"For the better, I'm assuming."

"Of course. If it wasn't, I would have let you know by now."

"Good. Anyway, shall we go take our seats now? It appears that the doors have finally opened."

She agreed and let him lead her through the beautiful hallways with their thick carpets, elegant chandeliers, vintage paintings, and flowers galore in the tall vases that lined the way. The whole atmosphere exuded one of money and class and she felt like a little girl again, stepping into this big people's world for a few moments in time.

As they waited for an usher to assist them in finding their seats, Megan turned to Ken. "So when are you going to let me in on how you got all this ready for today?"

"All in good time, Meg."

"But I want to know now! Tonight has been such a dream. First, the dinner. Now, the show. And another party afterward? How'd you manage it?"

"I didn't do it by myself, if that's what you're asking."

"No, that's not what I'm asking and you know it." She paused long enough to say 'excuse me' to the people already seated in their row as she led the way to their seats and sat down. "You know what I'm talking about."

"Yes, I do, but I can't say just yet. It's all a secret."

"Surely you can tell me at least one thing," she pleaded.

"Depends on what you want to know."

"How did you get tickets? You know I was practically devastated when I called and heard that they were sold out."

"Please, don't remind me. It was painful listening to you mope and complain how you thought you weren't going to be able to see this."

"I wasn't that bad, was I?"

"Worse," he smiled.

Megan rolled her eyes and dropped the subject, seeing that she wasn't going to get anywhere with him for the time being. At times, he could be just as stubborn as she. But, if she was meant to know, then it would come later. She glanced around. "Are we early or something?"

He looked at his watch. "Nope, not really. The show starts in twenty minutes."

"Only? You'd think there would be more people here by now, wouldn't you?"

"I don't know, Meg. You're the one who goes to this kind of stuff. Not me. Besides, it's a weekday. Maybe people aren't feeling up to it after a long day at a job."

"Maybe..." she replied, eyeing the empty, curtained stage in front of her. "But this show is a big deal. Surely there's got to be more people here tonight. Why else would the ticket office have told me it was sold out?"

"Here, why don't you look at this while we wait instead of wasting precious neurons in that head of yours on wondering?" Megan opened her mouth to retort but stopped to watch Ken pull something out from inside his jacket. Upon handing it to her, he started smiling when he saw Megan's eyes light up eagerly.

"Kenneth Gregory Rowe! When in the world did you get the program? I haven't left your side for more than five minutes tonight!" she cried out excitedly as she snatched the program from him. She paused after opening the cover though and looked back over at him. "You did not get this while I was in the restroom. This book has been autographed and personally addressed to me by the cast."

"You're right, I didn't get it while you were in the bathroom." She kept looking at him, waiting for him to explain but he wouldn't give in. "Don't even try, Meg. I'm not going to tell you until later."

Seeing that pestering him with questions wasn't getting her anywhere, she turned back to the program to start reading before the show started. She was so engrossed with her reading that she barely acknowledged the people who pardoned their way across her to get to their seat, nor noticed the man who sat down on the other side of her. She only knew that the show was about to start when the lights dimmed down, making it difficult to read. As she was settling into her seat however, she felt a hand tap lightly on her shoulder. Turning around, she found herself staring into a pair of dark eyes looking at her with something close to suspicion. "Excuse me miss, but may I see your ticket please?"

"Wha - Oh, sure." Despite thinking the situation a bit odd, Megan fumbled around in her purse a moment before drawing out the small piece of paper and handing it to the man. Large hands brought the ticket stub closer to his face in the dim light before handing it back to her. She heard him mumble an apology before sitting back down in the row behind her. Confused, Megan turned back around herself and finally took notice of the man beside her as he turned around for a quick whispered conversation. She found herself straining to listen in on their conversation and caught words like "security" and "safety" from the man behind them. The man sitting to her left spoke in tones too low for her to hear and she glanced curiously at Ken. Thoughts of the stranger sitting next to her flew out of her head when she found her companion fast asleep with his head down on his chest and she struggled to hold back a laugh. As the opening music started, Meg jabbed an elbow into his side, instantly waking him up. "No way are you going to sleep through your first show, mister. You're going to thank me for it later."

"I better," he whispered back. "I was having a good dream too."

"Goof," she smiled at him as the curtain rose to finally reveal the stage.

Twenty minutes into the show, she felt Ken poke her. "Be quiet, Megan. You're singing along and I want to watch this."

Meg smiled, happy that Ken was enjoying himself as much as she was. She made a mental note to herself to remind him of it next time she wanted to see another show but for the time being, she was content to just be where she was.

Ten minutes later, she felt another slight tap on her arm, this time coming from her left. "Excuse me, but you're still singing along."

This time she gave a quick look to her left, surprised at being caught by the stranger. Megan muttered an apology and clamped a hand over her mouth, thankful that the darkness of the theater hid her blush.

Soon though, the lights came back on in the theater for intermission and Ken excused himself to get some refreshments. "Do you want anything?"

"Thanks, but that's all right. I'm fine."

"All right then. I'll see you in a bit."

As Ken made his way out the row and out into the hall, Megan turned to the man who sat to her left. She waited a few minutes until he'd finished talking to person to his left before calling attention to herself. "Excuse me?" She waited for the man to turn his head toward her and for a moment she paused. For the first time that night, she got a clear look at the man who had taken the seat next to her and she was struck by a sense of familiarity. He wasn't the type she usually associated herself with though, quickly noting the short, light blonde hair and light blue eyes. She set the intrigue aside for now though. "I'd like to apologize for disturbing you earlier. I didn't even know I was singing along."

"Oh, that's all right. I didn't mind, but I think your companion was getting a little annoyed."

Megan gave a small laugh. "Honestly, I'm just glad he's enjoying himself. He was convinced he wasn't going to. What I really feel bad about is disturbing you tonight. I really should learn to be more mindful about the people around me."

The blonde-haired man gave a casual shrug. "Don't worry about it. I mean, look at who's sitting next to you tonight. There's your boyfriend and myself. Personally, I really don't mind. I actually think you've got a good voice."

Listening to him talk more, the feeling that she knew him from somewhere had grown. There was definitely something familiar about this man beside her but she was coming at a loss as to who he was. Even as Megan opened her mouth to reply though, Ken's voice let the two know that he was back. "Hey. Enjoying yourself so far?"

"Of course I am. Anyway, Ken, I'd like you to meet…" She paused and in that second, it clicked in her mind. She took in the blue eyes, the face, the deep, rich, and very familiar sounding voice… She remembered the whispered conversation from before the show and put it all together. The stranger had opened his mouth to answer for her but the hesitation was only a slight one and she introduced him as, "Jeffrey. Jeffrey, this is one of my best friends, Ken." Even as the two men shook hands, Meg's eyes never left the blue ones of her newer companion. The twinkling in their eyes let each other know the situation. For some reason, he was amused more than he was worried about the fact that she had recognized him. The fact that she was attempting to cover for him by using his middle name without him telling her to meant something – what that was, he wasn't quite sure but played along. He smiled in her direction.

"So what were you just talking about?"

"You," came Meg's reply.

"Good stuff, I hope."

"Always," she smiled sweetly in return.

"Actually, we were talking about her singing."

"Ahh, yes, and I was going to say how terrible I really am at singing. I can't even hold my own in choir anymore. If I was really good enough, I'd be the one up there on stage instead of just watching it from over here."

"Why do I get the feeling you're just being modest?"

"Please. We've just met. How can you tell?"

The blonde turned his attention the other man. "I actually consider myself a good judge of character and I think you're just hiding that talent of yours. What do you say, Ken?"

"You're right," he laughed.

"Fine. Just help him out there. You just see what happens when you try to get any help from me from your girlfriend." Megan gave a sly smile to "Jeffrey", who smiled back, genuinely amused that she'd now corrected his earlier assumption of them being a couple twice.

As Megan and Ken began to compare notes on the night's performance so far, "Jeffrey" flipped through Megan's program after asking to see it since he didn't know if he wanted one or not yet. Neither Ken nor Megan noticed the look he got in his eyes when he too came across the signatures inside. And neither noticed how, as the lights dimmed, he took out a pen and scribbled a little something in the program as well. In fact, once the second act was under way, Megan never noticed that she had begun to mouth along with the cast and failed to catch any of the times when the man to her left looked to her with a smile on his face.

Indeed, if she wasn't as intuned with the performance on stage, she would have noticed how he'd stopped paying attention to the stage altogether and just watched the intensity of her emotions play out across her face. He only realized that the production had ended when Megan stood up to applaud the cast. Quickly, he diverted his attention to the stage so he wouldn't be caught staring at her.

That forethought turned out to be unneeded though because even as the cast bowed out their final time, Ken turned to Megan and told her to wait there in her seat. Before she could ask why, he'd turned around and joined the mass of people slowly leaving the audience area.

Frowning a bit, she sat back down and tried looking for her program.

"Wondering where this went?"

Megan turned and was once again drawn into the man's eyes. "Yes, I am," she said, noticing the program in his hands. "Thank you," she said when he gave it back. "I'd forgotten you had it."

"No problem. Listen. Some friends and I are heading out tonight. Would you and Ken like to join us?"

"I'd love to, but I think we're already going out with some friends tonight."

"You think?"

Megan nodded. "I'm pretty sure. If it wasn't for that and the fact that I also have classes tomorrow, I would have loved to go with you."

"You're a student?"

"Yup. This fall, I start my last year in college

actually."

"Cool. Where at?"

Megan gave him the name of the college town thirty minutes away and answered his other questions while they waited for Ken to come back for her. The stranger found himself being drawn to this woman in front of him and he couldn't understand why. She was completely honest with him and that surprised him. The incident earlier had confirmed for him that she knew who he was and yet she wasn't trying to make herself sound more glamorous or anything like that. Her sincerity was attractive and it didn't hurt that she was beautiful to the eyes as well. He took in her warm, olive complexion, her wide, brown eyes, her long, slick hair – even without her gown, she would have stood out for him. But when she laughed? Often, he found his laughter mingling with hers in the few minutes they spent together before he looked down at his watch and groaned. "Hey look. It's been great meeting you, but I have to get going before I'm late. Besides, it looks like Ken is finally back for you."

Megan turned around and sure enough, her friend had just come back and was steadily coming their way. For some reason, she felt disappointed at seeing Ken coming closer. She wanted more time to talk with "Jeffrey". Before Ken could get within hearing range, she turned back to the other man. "Will I see you again?"

"Do you want to see me again?" the man smirked.

"Yes," Megan found herself saying. "I had a good time tonight."

"Then it's a promise. I'll see you again sometime," he said as he stood up.

"How though?"

"You're in college so that means you've got the smarts. I'm sure you'll find out some way. I do warn you that I leave by the end of the week though."

"Oh right. You have a tour you're supposed to be getting ready for, right?"

"So you do know who I am." He stated it as if it wasn't a question.

"Yes, I figured it out earlier but still! You're leaving it all up to me to do the work here. What about you?"

"You're the one who wants to see me again," he laughed.

"So what? Unless, of course," she started. "You mean that you didn't enjoy yourself tonight and this is your polite way of saying I'm never going to see you again."

He paused to look directly into her eyes. 'She really cuts to the quick, doesn't she,' he thought to himself before leaning in close to her, surprising her when she felt his warm breath fan her cheek as he whispered, "I really enjoyed your company tonight. Happy birthday, Megan. I really do hope to see you again soon."

He drew back as quickly and was already on his way out the aisle before she could call out, "Wait, how did you know my name?"

He turned around one last time. "You know mine. I'd say that's a fair enough trade for now. Nice meeting you, Ken."

"You too, Jeffrey," Ken waved from where he

stood next to Megan. "What was all that about?" he asked, turning to her.

"What was what about?" Megan asked, reluctantly breaking her gaze from the blonde's retreating back.

"You know what I'm talking about. What was Jeffrey just whispering to you just now?"

"Jeffrey?"

"Hello? Jeffrey. The guy who was just talking to you."

She blinked. "Oh yeah, Jeffrey. We weren't talking about anything."

"You're lying, Megan. The lights are up and you look like you're blushing a bit there," he grinned. "What's up with you?"

She smiled. "Nothing's up with me. I'm just happy."

He gave a mock sigh. "Fine, have it your way. You're the princess tonight and I should remember that. Anyway, let's get you to your golden carriage. There's a ball you should be attending," he said, taking her arm and leading her out of the theater.

2 | The Lost Boys

Ryan Jeffrey Garner turned to his fellow bandmate Joshua Butler as the two walked down their floor of the hotel. "So really, you liked it?" he was asking the tenor.

"Of course I liked it. I wouldn't just be saying something like that. And you know how I am. I'm not usually one to be into this kind of stuff, but after hearing all the hype about it and the good reviews, I had to check it out. I admit, the story line is a bit overused, being based on fairy tales and all, but everything else makes up for it. I'm just sorry I missed the cast here. I heard that it has some great people in it and I was a little upset I couldn't get any tickets."

"There were some empty seats last night," Ryan replied, thinking back.

"Really? I guess I should have gone with you then."

"But you said you were tired last night."

"I was, but once I got in, I couldn't go to sleep after I talked to Laurie so I just ended up renting some movies instead."

"Josh, the next time you say you're tired, remind me to just drag you along. You keep missing out when you insist on staying in."

"Oh please, Ryan. You make it sound like it's all my fault fun always happens when I'm not with you."

"That's because that's usually what happens and you know it."

"Uh huh, and you're just saying that to claim once again how much better off you are being the last bachelor of the group! Then tell me something. What made last night so much fun that I just had to be there?"

A female face flashed in Ryan's mind and the corners of his mouth curled upward. "Nothing," he said, quickly trying to suppress the unbidden memory. "I didn't mean it that way. I mean, you certainly found something to do last night in the end, but I still think that it would have just been better for you to get out instead of staying cooped up in here. You said so yourself that you would have liked to see the cast anyway and we're not staying here much longer before we're done with our shoot here," he finished lamely, inwardly groaning at himself.

His friend had caught the quick smile even when Ryan tried turning to hide it. Josh grinned. "Why, I do believe you're lying to me. You usually don't babble on like that. There was something else besides that show, wasn't there?"

"Of course not. After it ended, I went to hit the clubs with Matt and Connor, remember?"

"So something happened when you were with the guys?"

"No, nothing happened."

"Oh come on! We've known each other for awhile and you can't tell me what's making you so happy right now?"

"Is it that obvious?"

"Yes, it is. Now spill."

The sound of a door clicking open interrupted them and a new voice entered in on the conversation. "Ryan! I thought I heard you out here. What happened last night? You left us pretty quick. Hey Josh."

Josh gave Ryan a look. "Don't look at me like that! I said I went. I just didn't happen to stay very long."

"Did I just miss something here?" Matt, the third of their four member group, asked as he came out to join them.

"Not yet. He was just about to tell me what he was up to last night though."

"I wasn't up to anything at all!" Ryan protested.

"Then what are you hiding from us?"

"Nothing. I swear."

"You're lying. Even I can tell that much," Matt smiled, leaning casually against the wall and smiling at his friend's mild discomfort.

"There's nothing to lie about! I'm telling you the truth. I just had a good time at the musical, went to meet up with you and Connor, Matt, but I felt tired after so I came back here and went to bed. That's that!"

"Aah, so something did happen while you were at the show. I knew it!"

Ryan closed his eyes and groaned, his body sagging against his door. "How many times do I have to say this? No, nothing hap-"

"He met a girl," a gruff voice broke in. The three turned to see Ryan's bodyguard Reuben close by, watching in amusement.

Josh smacked himself on the forehead. "Of course! That explains why you're in such a good mood. Why couldn't I figure that out?"

"Cuz you young'uns can never see what's right in front of you," the older man laughed. "That or the celebrity status of being the hottest group on earth right now is getting to your heads."

"And you're always around to remind us of that, aren't you?" Matt smiled.

"Not always, but it comes as part of the job description. Keeps you guys grounded, you know?"

"Right," Josh smiled. "So what made this girl so special?" he asked, turning back to Ryan.

"Nothing…"

It was Matt's turn to moan while Reuben coughed, trying to smother more of his laughter. He wasn't being very successful. "All right. I wasn't here for most of the conversation, but even I am getting tired of hearing that word come out of your mouth. What gives, man? It's not like we won't find out anyway from Reuben, so why so secretive on us?"

"Because I don't know a thing about her!"

"What's her name?"

"Megan. And she's a college student around here," he quickly added when they looked like they wanted to prod him for more information.

"See? You do know something."

"You guys are impossible, you know that?"

"You keep saying that, but I don't think I'm impossible. What do you think, Matt?"

"Nope. I think I'm a very tolerable person.

Certainly not impossible. I think it's all in his mind."

Ryan just rolled his eyes. "Oh why do I put with you guys?"

"Because all of us together with Connor make some beautiful music together, and you're the big brother of the group, and you love us, and we love you," Matt stated with a cheeky grin. "Now tell us when you're going to see her again," Matt pressed.

"I don't know."

"What? Here you are all lovey dovey eyed and you don't even know when you're going to see her again? Didn't you get her number?"

"No... She has mine."

The light-hearted atmosphere suddenly changed and disappeared. Even Reuben looked suspicious. "Whoa... Ryan. Are you serious?" Joshua asked.

Matt nodded his head, also worried. "Yeah, Ryan. That's big stuff. You can't just give people your number. We have plenty of stalkers as it is. How can you trust this one?"

"I know, I know. Don't worry guys. I didn't exactly give her my number. She kinda has to find it first." His fellow bandmates stood there silently, confusion written all over both their faces. "Ahh, got you there, huh? Who's laughing now," he teased them but knowing he was doing nothing to ease their worries.

"Do we want to know?" Josh turned Matt.

"I think we've gotten as much as we're going to get from him for the moment," he replied, judging by Ryan's grin.

"Just one thing more then," Josh said.

"Maybe."

The brown-haired tenor with the hazel eyes took in a deep breath. "When do you find out?"

Ryan took out a cell phone from his pocket. "I find out when this phone rings and I hear her voice again." He tried to act casual about it, but his friends could tell that he was hoping for the best. "She said she wanted to see me again, and honestly, I want to see her again too. It's completely in her hands now, though..." He looked down at the phone, willing it to ring. When it didn't, he sighed. "What if-"

"Hey. You said she's in college, so she must be pretty smart. If you left her a clue, I'm sure she'll find it," Matt said, trying to ease Ryan's fears.

Instead of agreeing though, he gave an even sadder smile. "That's exactly what I told her last night. I just hope we're both right on this one. There's just something about her..."

3 | Happy Unbirthday

"Oh, I don't know. Just pick a CD," Megan was saying, never taking her eyes off the road as one of her co-workers from the hospital asked what she wanted to listen to. "I swear Ben, we go through this every time I give you a ride, wasting half the time it takes to go from the hospital to your place arguing about what I want to hear. You don't need to ask me. If it's in here, then that must mean I like it so I don't mind what you put in."

Ben's laughter filled the car. "You know you have fun every time we go through this. It loosens you up, you're happier, and therefore, I'm happy."

She smiled but didn't bother replying, glancing over to see him flipping through her CD's. A few moments later, music filled in the comfortable quiet that had settled around the two.

How can I prove to you, show to you, share with you
That my feelings are true?
How can I proclaim to the world that it took just one
glance
And I am now yours?

Megan hummed along with the tune as her mind worked overtime trying to figure out why the song sounded so familiar. "Hey Ben. What CD did you put in?"

"What? I'm shocked. I thought you knew all these boy bands by heart. Their songs, their names… Birthdays, favorite colors, marital status… You know, the usual diehard fan facts," he teased.

"Please, you make me sound like a teeny bopper. Those days are long gone."

"Yeah right! I still hear you playing stuff like TARJ in the background when I'm on the phone with you."

"Only sometimes."

"Right. Anyway, do you remember who sings this CD yet?"

"Well, you said it's of the boy band genre so it's down to the three or four groups I know of. And it's not TARJ, and it's not the B2B. The group sounds older, more mature, and the songs are more R&B-ish so I'm guessing it's Pulse."

"A long-winded explanation, but bingo! Took you long enough," he snickered.

"Ha-ha. It just happens to be that I haven't listened to this one in a long time."

"A week?"

"Very funny. Remind me that next time you ask for I ride, I shouldn't give you one. Besides, you live on the other side of town. You're out of my way. I don't know why I bother driving you around," she said as she pulled up in front of his apartment.

"Oh come on! You know I'm just playing."

"Oh sure. You always stop teasing me once I start threatening to leave you behind. No way is that angel face of yours going to convince me otherwise."

Ben laughed as he stepped out of the car and

reached into the back for his backpack. "Ahh, Megan. You're getting to know me too well. Anyway, want to come in for awhile?"

"I would but I can't. I've got a lot to get done tonight."

"As always. You know, you ruin the image of slacker college students everywhere."

"I try my best," she grinned. "I'll see you next week though, right?"

"Of course. My turn to drive."

"Uh huh. I'll see you then."

"Sure. Take care and drive safe now," he said before shutting the door behind him.

With a final wave, she drove off back the way she came, still humming along with the music of Pulse's first album for another few minutes before pulling into her driveway. Shutting off the engine and gathering her backpack from the back, she found herself going back to the first song that they'd listened to in the car and began softly singing more of what she remembered.

If I had all the wealth in the world,
I would lay it all at your feet
Just to show you how I'd give my all to you.

Megan smiled as she went to the mailbox to see if there was any mail, remembering the time when she and her best friend had written fan-fiction and that the song she was still humming to was one of the songs they'd used in some story. Glancing through the pile in her hand, she only found the usual ads and quickly put them all in the recycling bin before turning to the front door. Before she could even put her key in the lock though, the door burst wide open and she found one of her roommates holding the door open for her with one hand and trying to put on a shoe with the other. "Hey Kathy. School, work, or internship?" she asked.

"Work. One of my friends and I switched days this week and I totally forgot until now and I have to be there in five minutes."

"Gotcha. Don't get into any accidents when driving over."

"You know me. I'll try not to. I'll see you tonight though, okay? Later!"

"Bye," Megan waved as Kathy grabbed her keys and sped down the walkway on the way to her car.

Shutting the door behind her, Megan moved to her own bedroom at the end of the hallway. She hesitated there, seeing a piece of paper taped to her door. Taking that off, she opened her bedroom door and read the note that let her know that her last two roommates wouldn't be getting in until later that night also. As she crossed the room to put the note in the trash, a voice startled her. "About time you got home. I was wondering if I was going to have the house all to myself tonight."

Megan whirled around and was greeted by a familiar face. "Lori!" The two embraced in a long hug, laughing for no reason at all. Megan's smile was still wide on her face when she drew back a minute later. "Oh my God, Lori! I was just thinking of you! I can't believe you're here!"

"Well believe it. I'm really here."

Megan stared at the best friend she hadn't seen in half a year. "It can't be! The Lori I know is back on the east coast interning for some big company for the entire summer."

"Not quite the entire summer. I neglected to let you know that I had a few days of vacation before that starts so I decided to come out here and surprise you for your birthday."

"A few days a little late, don't you think?" Meg teased.

"Unbirthday then. Don't complain. Otherwise, I may just fly back and leave you alone."

"Don't even think about it. Come on. Why don't I fix us up some dinner and you can update me on everything that's been going on." Megan shrugged off her backpack and placed it next to her desk before leading the way back out to the kitchen. "Pasta okay?" Lori nodded that it would be fine so she took out a pot to start boiling some water. "So spill already. How'd you manage to keep this a secret from me?"

"As if I would really ruin the surprise. What do you think of me?"

Megan smiled. "You're a wonderful best friend whom I love lots and lots."

"Nice one."

"I try. Now tell me everything."

"Not yet. I want to hear what I missed on Monday."

"No! It'll take too long."

"And you think my side of the story would be any shorter? Relax. I'm not leaving anytime soon so start talking."

"Oh fine, have it your way like you always do." Lori gave Megan a mischievous grin as she waited for the details to be given, and Megan spared no cost in accounting everything that happened that magical night for her. She went through the details of her day spent with family and relatives, the huge dinner with everyone who could make it, going to the theater with Ken, and then the dancing afterward for those who still didn't want to end the night. "It was funny. I mean, when he said carriage, I didn't expect a real horse-drawn carriage to be outside waiting for us. I thought it was going to be just the limo again, but no! It was nice though. There were blankets to keep out the chill as we went through downtown."

Lori laughed. "Oh, that must have been a sight. I'm so sorry I missed it."

"Don't worry. Dad was there with his video camera taping our arrival. He spent most of the day behind that thing, actually. You'd think it was some big occasion."

"Stop making it sound as if it wasn't, Meg. You only turn twenty-one once in a lifetime, and-"

"And you guys just couldn't wait to spoil me, huh?" she laughed.

"After all these years, don't you know by now that it's not nice to interrupt other people, especially best friends like me? As I was saying, you never had a sweet sixteen party or been the focus of a cotillion. You never got the experience of being treated as a princess and we all thought why wait?"

"But after this year, what will I have to look forward to now for my birthdays? I don't want the whole anti-climax thing to happen to me."

"Then we won't let that happen. If we can't think of anything else, we could go back to old days and just take you to a certain kiddie pizza place again."

Megan looked up from her plate and made a face. "Thanks but no. I've had enough of revisiting my childhood that way. It'd make me feel older than I already am."

"Sweetie, that's the idea," she laughed.

Meg just rolled her eyes and stood up to stretch a little. "Done?"

"Sure. Here, let me give you a hand."

The two gathered their things and went to the sink to wash the dishes while they continued their talk. "So is that all that happened? Just fun and more fun? No special guy that you've neglected to tell me about or other new twists to your romantic life?"

"Well…"

"Hah! I knew it! You were holding out on me."

"I wasn't holding out. I just didn't know how to bring it up."

"Anyway…" Lori gave her best friend a look.

"There was this guy…" Lori rolled her eyes and Meg smiled. "He was at the theater. I didn't even notice him at first because I was talking to Ken, but then this guy behind me asked to see my ticket." She paused at Lori's look. "I know. I didn't get it at first either. He glanced at it and gave it back and while I was turning back around, I finally noticed that someone had sat in the seat next to me on my left. I didn't really notice him then either, but he kinda noticed me because I was supposedly singing along.

Don't laugh, Lori. I was so embarrassed! I tried stopping when Ken told me the first time I was singing along, but further in, he let me know I was doing it again. Anyway, I waited until intermission to talk to him, but I had to wait a few minutes since he was talking to someone else. So there I am trying not to seem rude and stare or listen in on their conversation, but I was also getting my first real good look of him and-"

"Let me guess. He took your breath away," Lori interrupted, a gleam in her eyes as she tried not to laugh.

"Funny, but no. To be honest, he didn't impress me that way at first. I was actually just wondering why he looked so familiar. There was just something about him that seemed to remind me of someone."

"Hmm... Someone you knew in another lifetime or not?"

"You know, that didn't even come across my mind. It was definitely from this lifetime, I was sure. It wasn't until we started talking for a few minutes that it clicked for me. I mean, come on! You'd think I'd be able to place any old blonde-haired, blue-eyed guy I've met in the past since there are just so few of them out there that I've really talked to."

"Ooh... Megan! What happened to your seemingly specific taste for only Asian guys on the market? I thought any guy with blue eyes was off limits for you," she teased.

"Oh stop it," she laughed in return. "Just because I haven't met anyone who's been worth my time that fits that description doesn't mean they're off limits for me, and anyway, that's all beside the point."

"And the point would be..."

"I'll get to it but first, do you need to take a shower?"

"No, it's okay. I just need to freshen up and change into my pajamas."

"Me too. Why don't you go ahead and use my bathroom, and I'll just go take a quick shower in the other bathroom?"

"Are you sure this isn't just a ploy to stall for time and leave me wondering what the hell happened to you that night?"

"Of course not. What do you think of me?" she laughed. Lori just shook her head and gathered her things for the bathroom. Megan followed suit and was soon trying to wash away all the strain she'd gotten from another long day. For a few minutes, she tried to relax, but a pair of blue eyes haunted her thoughts and wouldn't leave. By the time she stepped out of the bathroom, a tired frown on her face just wouldn't leave. As she thought, Lori was already done and sitting in the chair at her desk waiting for her when she stepped back into her room, closing the door after her. "You know, you should be glad I don't have too much work to do before tomorrow. I have a feeling we're going to be up late."

"As always," Lori answered, a worried frown forming to match her friend's. "What's wrong?"

"Nothing. I'm just thinking about something."

"Then think out loud then. I can't mind read."

"Oh come on. You could always tell what was on

my mind before. Anyway, I'll get to it. Want to take the trundle bed or is a sleeping bag fine?" As soon as the sleeping situation had been decided, Megan made the way to her own bed and lay down, clutching a pillow.

Megan finally noticed the soft music playing in the background and glanced over to her CD player. "I hope you don't mind. I just wanted to listen to something while waiting for you."

Megan finally gave a small smile. "No problem. Interesting choice though. Anyway, what have I told you about the guy so far?"

"Only that he's blonde-haired and blue-eyed."

"Add deep voice then."

Lori cracked a smile. "What's with you and guys with deep voices? I mean, there was your first boyfriend and practically everyone else you've gone out with. Except for what's his name, your friend here. He's the only exception and I've always wondered why. There's just something about having a deep, sexy voice that seems to turn you on."

Megan smiled. "So I have a thing for baritones and basses. Is that such a crime?"

"No, but what will be a crime is you holding out on me much longer."

"So the patience is wearing thin."

"Megan!"

"All right, all right," she laughed. "Do you remember the group we're listening to right now?"

"Yeah, it's Pulse. I picked it out of the stack."

"Who has a low voice in the group?"

"Connor."

Megan rolled her eyes. "Even after all this time, you go for your hottie, don't you?" she laughed, referring to their time writing about their favorite boy band members in college. "Anyway, who's voice is deeper than Connor?"

"Ryan is the actual bass in the group. What? Did the guy sound like him? Look like him? He wasn't..." Megan gave her a look. "You're not making me think what I think you're making me think." Her friend still wouldn't do anything else but give a smile and shrug. "Oh my God, Meg! You met Ryan Garner of Pulse!? Why didn't you just tell me this in the first place!"

"Because I like building up the story and seeing how you'd react?" she shrugged. "Besides, that's not the end of my problems."

"What problems could there be? I'm assuming you guys hit it off by the look on your face."

"That's a definite yes. Oh my God, Lori, he was so sweet and funny, polite and everything. There were no awkward moments except for the beginning when I was trying to say sorry and failing at it. But after that, things just clicked between us. Maybe I'm making something out of the probably twenty minutes we spent talking with each other, but the fact that we could talk so easily... I can't just do that with guys, and even my close guy friends and I have those moments where there's just dead time."

"That's great. So have you seen him since?"

"Not exactly..."

"Meg, please tell me you did 'not' just set yourself up here."

"I'm trying to make myself believe that. So here's the dilemma. The fact is I asked him if we could see each other again, and he said yes. I asked how, and he said it was all up to me. He said I had the brains and if I thought about it long and hard enough, I'd come up with the solution. To add to that, he let me know that he leaves by the end of this week, so I have a deadline on my head, and I still haven't come up with how to get in touch with him."

"Leave it to the guys, famous or not, to make us women worry so much."

She nodded. "And it's not like I haven't tried. My purse was right next to me on my seat, between Ken and I, the entire time so he couldn't have gone through that and left a slip of paper there. I looked anyway. The only other thing I had left was my program, but that was-"

Megan trailed off, a faraway look in her eyes and Lori got the hint. "Where's the program now?"

"I totally forgot that I let him take a look at it for a bit." Megan scrambled off her bed and into her closet. "I put it here with all my other programs," came her muffled reply. "I just don't see how he could have left anything..." She brought it out triumphantly.

"Unless he wrote in it himself," Lori pointed out.

Megan smacked herself on the head. "Oh my God, I'm so stupid. Why didn't I think of that?"

Lori grinned. "Because you were blinded by love. Anyway, that's what I'm here for. Now open it already and let's see if we can't find what we need to find."

4 | Crying Wolf

Ryan's room was... Well to put it quite frankly, it was a mess. To say that a hurricane or tornado had blown through would put things mildly. The furniture had been moved about to make room for the guys when they'd come in for a crash writing session and was never quite the same afterward... Not only were wrinkled clothes scattered everywhere, but a mess of papers were strewn about, hopelessly out of any semblance of order. Candy wrappers, some with candy still half eaten in them, and other snacks littered the floor. A stack of videos lay by the door because Ryan had offered to return them for Josh. One of Connor's hats lay nearby as well, forgotten and lost in the clutter. A gaming console and some video games were in a pile where the TV should have been but which was now buried under a pile of clothes. Why his clothes were all about the room was a wonder.

And Ryan wasn't looking any better himself. He was half in and half out of a suit. His glossy, black shoes were untied, laces dragging behind him. His shirt was untucked and a black tie hung at his neck, still waiting to be tied. A frown was on his face as he left the bathroom and faced the rest of the suite, surveying the damage he and his friends had made in the few days they'd been there. When he couldn't find a clock, he glanced at his watch to see how much time he had. Shaking his head, he took in a deep breath and began sorting through everything in search of his dinner jacket.

Slowly but surely, his room began to take shape again. He'd gathered all of the clothes together into a big pile by the closet, moved all the furniture back to where he thought they belonged, and was only starting to gather up the papers and trash when he heard a phone ring. On instinct, he looked over to the hotel phone he'd only recently unearthed and knew already that wasn't the source of the ringing. As the ringing continued, he tried desperately to place where his cell phone might have been put and in a second, his eyes glanced over to the large pile of clothes he'd just assembled. Groaning, he raced for the pile and began throwing things about again in search for the phone. 'It might finally be her calling,' was the first thought that crossed his mind as he moved from wrinkled piece of clothing to another. "How the hell did I manage to get this stuff all over the place?" he muttered to himself.

He was halfway through the pile of clothes already when he realized that the sound had moved over to the pile that he'd just looked through. Groaning a little, he turned around and began to slowly go through all of his clothes, this time checking each pocket. Surprisingly, the phone was still ringing by the time he answered it. "Hello?"

"Hey Ryan! What took so long? I thought you'd never pick up!"

"It's a wonder I found the phone at all with the mess you and the guys left, Connor."

"Oops. We did kinda leave things out of order,

huh?"

"You can say that again. I've been straightening up for," he glanced at his watch. "Half an hour now and it's still pretty bad."

"Look, sorry man. We didn't mean to."

"I know. It's okay. But just to let you know, you guys left some stuff behind, including one of your hats."

"Huh. I was wondering where that went. Thanks, man. I'll pick it up from your place next time I see you."

"Sure. Anyway, I gotta get going. I want to get things straightened up some more before I have to go to that dress rehearsal."

"No problem. I just wanted to call and say hey and ask if she called yet."

Ryan paused. "She?"

His friend caught the uncomfortable sound in his voice. "Sorry, man. I didn't know. I mean, I was just curious and wanted to know since I know you like her and all and I was hoping for the best and…" He paused to take a breath. "I'm rambling, aren't I?"

Ryan gave a slight chuckle. "Yeah, you are, and I'm sorry to stop you as amusing as it is but I really should get going. I still have to finish getting ready."

"Right. No problem. I'll let you go then."

"Okay. I'll see you in a few days, okay?"

"Sure. Take care now."

"Yeah. You too."

Tucking the phone in his pocket after hanging up, he turned back to the pile of clothes to begin his quest for his dinner jacket. "I hope it's not wrinkled," he muttered to himself as he pawed through the pile further. Soon, he drew it out and sighed in dismay when he saw it its sorry state. "Just my luck." Just then, the phone began to ring again. "Hello?"

"Ryan?"

"Hey Matt. What's up?"

"Nothing. I just wanted to let you know we're back already."

"I figured as much already. Connor just called a few minutes ago."

"Really? Huh. He didn't tell me he was calling you."

"Well he did. He was wondering if Megan called or not."

"Oh. Well... Did she?"

"Who? Megan?"

"Well yeah. Did she call yet?"

"No, but I will tell you one thing."

"What's that?"

"I'm going to be late to dress rehearsal if I keep talking to you. No offense man, but I still have to find a jacket to wear. My dinner jacket's wrinkled."

"Sorry, Ryan. We didn't mean to trash your room like that."

"It's all right. I just have to really get going now, okay?"

"No problem. I'll talk to you later."

Once again, Ryan tucked his phone away as he combed through the clothes, trying to find something suitable to wear. Just as he was about to give up though, out of the corner of his eye, he spotted one of Josh's leather jackets. After glancing at it to make sure there were no spills and that it was presentable enough, he shrugged it on and trekked back into the bathroom. He ran a brush through his hair, straightened and tucked in his shirt, fixed his tie… He was bending down to tie his shoes when his phone rang. "Ryan here."

"It's Reuben."

"Hey. Anything wrong?"

"Nope. Just checking up on my charge and making sure you're not getting into any trouble while I'm away."

Ryan laughed. "Don't worry. I'm fine. I'm just rushing around trying to get ready."

"Oh yeah! That dress rehearsal's soon, huh?"

"Yeah, and it's just my luck that now's the time people feel the need to call me."

"Hey, hey. I get the picture. I just wanted to remind you to stay out of trouble and to ask if you got any phone calls yet."

"Only from you, Matt, and Connor. What's this? You all curious about the girl?"

"Hey, I was there and I saw you checking her out. I just wanted to know."

"And when she does call, I'll let you all know. Right now, I just have to get going."

"Okay man. I'll see you when you get back. It's weird not being around you though, watching your back and all."

"I know, but the video shoot's done and at least without the guys, I'm less noticeable."

"Right. You be careful anyway."

"Of course. Later."

Ryan glanced at his watch and groaned. He

looked at himself once more in the mirror and dashed out the door, locking it securely behind him. Impatiently, he waited for the elevator to come up to his floor. He began pacing as the elevator descended to the bottom level. He was thankful when the bellhop waved down a taxi for him even as he put on his sunglasses and added a cap in an attempt to hide his identity as best he could, but his irritation came back when he realized he was stuck in traffic. Seeing as he wasn't going to get to the church in time, he called ahead to let them know where he was. Just as he hung up though, a familiar ring sounded in that cab. "Yeah?"

"Whoa, Ryan. Don't bite my head off. I just wanted to say hi."

"Sorry, Josh. It's just been a long afternoon."

"I can tell. I just wanted to let you know I got home safe and I was wondering…" He trailed off.

"Let me guess. You're wondering if Megan has called yet."

"How'd you know?" Surprise rang in his voice.

"The other guys and Reuben called asking the same thing, but to answer your unasked question, no, she hasn't called."

"Oh, all right. I just hope that she didn't try calling while we were talking to you. That'd just be your luck, huh?"

"Don't jinx it, man! I didn't even think about that!"

"Oops. Sorry. I guess I should let you go then, huh?"

"Yeah, that'd be a good idea. I'm just getting out at the church now anyway."

"All right. Talk to you later then."

Ryan stepped out of the yellow car and reached in to pay the driver before turning to the church in front of him. He ignored the traffic of vehicles behind him and the wave of people going around him as he stared at the church's simple facade. Taking in a deep breath, he strode to the waiting doors. Before he could open them though, above the noise of the crowd, he heard his phone go off once more. Muttering to himself, he picked it up. "Hello?" he heard himself bark.

He heard a short gasp. "Oh, I'm so sorry. I think I have the wrong number," a female voice rushed.

"Wait! Hello?" Ryan prayed that she hadn't hung up.

"Jeffrey? Oh god. I mean... Is this Ryan?"

Without meaning to, his mouth crept up into the first smile he'd had all afternoon. "Yes, this is Ryan. How are you, Megan?"

5 | Happily Ever After

"All right, Lori. Be honest. How do I look?" Megan carefully made her way out of the bathroom and into her bedroom to await her best friend's criticism.

Lori was silent as she was looked over with a critical eye. "Turn around."

Megan did as she was told and waited some more, trying to read her friend's expression. "Well?" she asked when still nothing came out of her mouth. "What?" A hint of worry crept into her voice when Lori took her hand and brought her out into the dining room.

"Sit down. I want to try something with your hair."

"What!?" she screeched. "It's…" She glanced at a nearby clock. "Almost two. He's going to be by here any minute now to pick me up!"

"Stop stressing, Meg! There's still half an hour left and that leaves me plenty of time to play with your hair. Geez, you've been a nut since you called him yesterday."

"Can you blame me? I was so certain he'd already be gone."

"Well you're lucky he's not. Now hold still while I try this."

Megan settled into the chair and took in a few deep breaths, trying to calm the fluttering in her heart and stomach. "Am I crazy?"

"Hmm?"

"To be doing this, going out with Ryan after we've only met one time? I mean, what was I thinking when I talked to him on Monday? Wait, I take that back. I wasn't thinking. That's it. Oh god, I must have sounded so stupid to him, so ordinary. I'm sure he's heard my story before. What makes me so special? What if-"

"Stop!" Lori almost screamed, startling Megan from her ranting. "And hold still! You're fidgeting again. That's better," she said, when Megan calmed down again. "Now Meg, I wouldn't be doing your hair and helping you out like this if I didn't think it was a good idea now, would I?"

"Lori, you don't know if this is a good idea any more than I do. For all we know, he could be the exact opposite of what we hear in the media. I mean, what if he's not what he seems?"

"You're the one who met him and talked to him. Did you get any bad feelings from him when you talked?"

"No…"

"Then I wouldn't think that will be a problem with you two. You're a good judge of character. Give him a chance."

"What if I'm not what he thinks I am though? I mean, look at me!"

"I am looking and I love what I see! What guy, super mega pop star or not, wouldn't agree? Meg, don't be putting yourself down so much. You're smart, and nice, and friendly."

"You're also my best friend and therefore, have a

very biased opinion," she kidded back before groaning. "He's surely surrounded by all these gorgeous girls out there and could easily just pick any of them."

"But he didn't pick just any of them. He picked you to be his date for this wedding he's part of. Think about it. He's probably constantly hounded by all these women who put on airs to be in his good graces and get close to him. Don't you think he's tired of being around people like that who treat him special for what he is to the public?"

"I know, I know. We've been through this over and over already," she sighed. "I'm just scared. I've never done anything like this before."

"And that's exactly why you should do it, otherwise you'll live a lifetime of regrets. What have you got to lose?" She handed a mirror to Megan so she could look at herself now. Lori had taken all of her hair out of the high ponytail she'd had earlier and tousled it to give it some life. Without bothering for a comb or brush, she put half her hair up in a half ponytail, twisting and letting the ends fall naturally. The new look was definitely fun and stylish, something that usually didn't match a wedding scene, but Ryan had said that it wasn't a really formal occasion either... So what was she worried about?

Megan looked away from the mirror and smiled. "Thanks, Lori. It looks great." She got up to give her a hug, half in thanks and half to hide her still worried frown. 'What do I have to lose? There's always my heart, Lori. Always my heart.'

- - -

Knock, knock, knock.

It wasn't that much longer after Lori had finished with Megan that there was a rapping at the front door. Megan quickly glanced at it and then back down to her watch. "He's a little early," she said as she got up to answer the door. "You know, I still feel bad about going out like this. This is your vacation after all," she said, turning to Lori before opening the front door.

"Don't worry about it. You going off just gives me incentive to do something else tonight."

"Oh yeah? Like what?"

"Well I haven't quite figured that out yet."

"I didn't think so. Anyway, I've got to go. We'll talk when I'm back." A nervous grin formed on her face as she finally pulled open the door. "You're…" She stopped. The man at her front door was dressed in a suit all right, but instead of Ryan, she found herself looking up into an elderly man's face. "I'm sorry. You're not who I was expecting. May I help you?"

"I'm looking for Megan," the man replied.

"I'm Megan."

"Mr. Garner was running a little behind schedule and requested to have you picked up first," he explained, answering her unasked question. "If you'll just follow me to the car then," he said, turning to lead the way.

Meg indicated for Lori to lock up after her before she rushed to catch up to the stranger, slipping into the back seat of the car when he opened the door for her.

The ride into the city was pretty much a silent one as the driver sang along with the radio. Meg tried to listen along since this was a station she never listened to. A girl was singing about some blue-eyed boy she'd just met and fallen in love with. 'How ironic,' she thought to herself. 'The music I listen to always has a knack for mirroring what's going on in my life that moment, huh?' She sighed and turned to stare out the window. Without Lori to talk to, and now a song that encompassed all she was feeling right now playing on the ride over, her worries come back triple-fold. She couldn't deny the fact that she was genuinely attracted to Ryan now that she'd met him, even beyond her initial liking him when she just knew him as a member of Pulse. She knew better than to hide that from herself anymore, but her desire to see Ryan again to make sure that her birthday hadn't been a fantasy was quickly being overcome by her fear of making a fool of herself. She could just imagine herself tripping over her feet, spilling her food, or saying the wrong thing and insulting someone unintentionally. With each minute that passed, the worse the situations became in her head, and Megan's doubts grew until she had convinced herself that this was all a mistake.

Megan was so compelled to tell the driver to just turn back around that it was only then that she realized she was already in the city and they were now parking in front of a hotel. Immediately, Meg's heart quickened even more. There was no chance to go now that the car was stopped. Her driver had rolled down his window and was having a quick, low conversation with a uniformed man outside. That man tipped his hat upon seeing her and walked away. She knew it would be embarrassing if she'd just opened the door and walked away, but the thought tempted her nonetheless. Megan forced herself to sit still and looked down into her hands. They were cold to the touch and gripped tight around her purse, sure signs that she was nervous. She missed the amused look the driver gave her when he glanced up into the rearview mirror to see why his guest was so quiet. "Is anything the matter, miss?"

Meg almost jumped in her seat. She'd been so lost in her thoughts she had almost forgotten about him. "I'm sorry?"

The man smiled back at her. "I was just asking if anything was the matter. You look worried. If it's Mr. Garner, you needn't worry. He'll be down soon."

"Great. I can't wait," she tried to smile back but even to her ears, it sounded like she was forcing herself to be chipper.

"What's wrong? Shouldn't that be a good thing? I would have thought that you would like to spend the extra time with him seeing as he's never around these parts that often."

"Well," she started, hesitating. "Actually, we just met on Monday."

She noticed the look of surprise on his face. "Oh…"

"Yes, we ended up sitting next to each other at a

show and-."

He raised a hand to stop her. "No need to explain, miss. It's between you two, and I'm just the driver," he smiled. Megan looked at the man closer, noting that his eyes were twinkling with kind laughter. 'Why, he could be one of those store Santa's in the Christmas season,' she thought to herself and found herself smiling back in return and relaxing a little bit in her seat. "There now. I told you not to worry."

"I'm sorry. I'm just a little anxious I guess," she ended up saying.

"That's understandable dear, but don't worry. Mr. Garner doesn't bite. I'm sure the two of you will get along just fine."

The two shared a smile and not long afterward, the door to her left swung open and a breathless man settled in next to her, sunglasses and hat pulled down tight to hide his face. "Hurry, Charles! There's only an hour until the ceremony and I'm supposed to be helping!"

"It's your fault for sleeping in so late, Mr. Garner," the driver laughed as they pulled out into the stream of moving cars.

Ryan turned his attention to his companion as he took off the cap and ran a hand through his hair. "Hey," he smiled, taking off his sunglasses too.

"Hi," she smiled back.

"Thanks for coming on such short notice."

"No problem. I'm glad you invited me. I just wish I had more time to get ready though. I'm not used to doing things at the last minute."

"Well, you know you would have been more

prepared if you had called earlier instead of just yesterday."

"And I told you that you were overestimating my intelligence," she joked.

"I'm sure that you're just saying that."

"Oh really? What makes you so sure?"

"Well, I was right when I said you could sing well, wasn't I?"

Megan laughed and Ryan relaxed into his seat, clearly enjoying this. "How in the world can you compare singing with being smart?"

"Well in the music business, the two go hand in hand. You can't be successful if you don't know what you're doing."

"But I'm not in the business," she pointed out. "Try again."

"You could be in the business."

"Uh uh. No way are you changing the subject. I already told you I'm no good."

"And I don't believe you."

"What will it take to prove I'm right?"

Ryan looked at her thoughtfully for a moment, a small smile on his face. "Well, the only thing I can think of is for you to sing not only for me but for an unbiased group of critics, aka, my friends who don't know your talent just yet."

"Yeah right! You've got to be kidding."

"I'm serious. The only way to prove if either one of us is right is for you to sing your heart out."

"Well then you're out of luck. There's no way I'm going to sing like that in front of people I don't know."

"I'm assuming you've sung in front of audiences

47

before. What makes this any different?"

"I always end up singing as part of a big choir, that's what's different. It's been a long time since I've tried any solo stuff, and that was in high school!"

"Right. Three years can't make that much difference."

She looked at him in surprise. "You remembered what year of college I'm in? I'm impressed."

He beamed at her compliment. "Don't underestimate me just because I'm a guy. I do listen, especially to beautiful women who've just had their twenty-first birthday."

"How'd you know that?"

"I looked in your program, remember? How else would I have known to say happy birthday to you?"

"I don't know," Megan said, looking at him in a new light. "It's just so weird because people usually don't remember my birthday since it's in the summer, and here you are not only remembering that but how old I am." She shook her head, still surprised. "Anyway, what does this have to do with solo singing?"

He smiled. "Absolutely nothing. I just feel like I got to know you that much better."

Megan rolled her eyes. "I don't see how you could. I haven't told you anything that you didn't know already," but she was smiling as she said so. "So where is this wedding anyway?"

"We're almost there actually. You can see it for yourself when we round this corner."

They'd left the hustle and bustle of downtown and were in one of the quieter, more homely neighborhoods of the city. A small church came into view and she could see the guests walking into or milling about the entranceway. "There are a lot of people. Can we all fit in there?" she asked after counting the number of people she'd seen.

He grinned. "Surprisingly, yes."

Before she could ask anymore questions, the car stopped and the door opened for her. It was a beautiful afternoon, picture perfect for any wedding. Birds chirped from above in the surrounding trees, puffy white clouds speckled the dazzling blue sky, and the sun shone warmly on this festive occasion. Still, she had just barely enough time to take in a breath of the fresh air before she felt Ryan take her by the arm and lead her inside. And just as quickly, he excused himself, leaving her alone so he could help where he was needed. Another man ushered her into one of the pews and beckoned for her to sit down before turning to greet and seat more guests. In a few minutes, the ceremony started and she watched as Ryan walked the bride down the aisle to her beau.

For the first time that day, Megan finally gave herself the opportunity to look at Ryan. Seeing him up close and in person was definitely a different experience than watching him on TV. Ryan's blonde hair was groomed and cut short. He was clean shaven – always a bonus in her eyes. His broad shoulders and sculpted chest from all the working out he and his bandmates did to stay in shape were covered in a well-fitting tailored suit on top of matching slacks. But his smile and his twinkling blue eyes – Megan couldn't seem to keep her heart beating normally, and she wasn't sure if it was because of her being a fan or more.

The rest of the wedding flew by, ending happily as all weddings should. As people drifted out to wish their best to the newlywed couple, Megan stayed seated and looked around her. The church was simple, devoid of the normal, gloomy images of patron saints passing judgment on those who looked up on them. Also absent were the elaborate settings that usually decorated the front of the church. No marble or other precious metal adorned the altar or any of the other furniture in front. The sunlight that filtered in through all the open windows and doors further brightened up the place, leaving a light and cheerful atmosphere to compliment this day.

Megan closed her eyes and played back the wedding in her mind. There had been no mishaps, save for the slight misplacement of the rings. She chuckled. But that didn't ruin anything. Everything felt so right. Everyone was so happy. And the bride and groom were so evidently in love with each other. 'Those two look to deserve all the best they can get.' She sighed. 'The perfect wedding. I wonder if that day will ever come for me.'

"A penny for your thoughts?" a voice whispered into her ear and she shivered slightly, feeling the warmth of his breath tickle her skin.

Lazily, she opened her eyes and found Ryan still leaning close to her, a smile playing on his lips. "What? Are my thoughts worth so little to you?" she smiled, teasing him.

"More actually, but I'm afraid we have no time

for that now. It's time we get going to the reception. Annie and Michael are almost done with pictures and we need to be there to greet them at the reception." With that, Ryan reached for one of her hands and drew her to her feet before leading the way out to where Charles was waiting for them.

6 | The Banquet

Meg found herself cheering along with everyone else when the newlyweds finally arrived at the reception hall and more pictures were taken. After a few minutes of chatting, the groom announced that dinner was to be served, leading the flock of people into the dinner hall. Meg protested when Ryan tried to steer her to the head table. "I can't sit up there with you! I don't know anyone!"

"Stop fussing, Meg," he smiled. "You're my guest and as my guest, you have to sit by me. I won't have you sitting by yourself in a lonely corner of the room where you'd definitely not know anyone. Now sit," he finished, pulling out her chair for her. Grumbling, she sat. "And none of that either, Meg. Being at the head table means that you have to mind your manners and set an example for the other guests."

"You're loving this, aren't you?"

"Loving what?" he asked, turning innocent blue eyes to her. A devilish grin spread across his face. "I'm just reminding you to mind your manners," he added with a hearty laugh.

"What am I missing?" a female voice intruded in their conversation.

Ryan found himself quickly back up on his feet, greeting the new bride with a bear hug. "Annie! How does marriage feel for you so far?"

She laughed. "It hasn't been an hour yet, Ryan.

What do you expect? I'm still reeling from all the pictures we're taking. I swear, I'll need at least a week to recover from all these flashes from those cameras."

"Be thankful you're only getting it today. For me, it's such a welcome relief to not be the one in the spotlight for once. Try dealing with it on a more daily basis."

"Thanks, but I'll pass. So Ryan, aren't you going to introduce me to this lovely woman beside you?"

"Where are my manners? Of course, Annie. Annie, this is Megan. Megan, meet Annie."

"It's a pleasure to meet you," Megan said, shyly.

"The pleasure's all mine. To be honest, I'm glad he," she said, pointing to the man who sat between the two at the table, "chose you as his guest. I was worried that he may have brought Charles up here with him."

"He's not a bad guy."

"No, you're right. Charles is a perfect gentleman compared to you, Ryan, who has the gall to tease me on my wedding day." She paused to give Ryan a look before turning back to Megan. "No, Charles is a nice enough man. It just wouldn't have been as much fun sitting with Charles as it is watching Ryan trying to win a woman's heart." Megan and Ryan both blushed while Annie smiled and nodded to herself. "I knew it. Listen, Megan. If Ryan here ever does anything wrong, let me know and I can help kick his behind for you. Knowing him for as long as I have, it's one of my privileges, and I welcome any opportunity to remind him of his roots."

Meg laughed. "I don't think that will be necessary. He's been a gentleman so far, but I will keep it in mind in case the occasion ever comes up."

"Hey! That's not fair, Annie!" Ryan moaned.

"All is fair in love and war, Ryan. You should know that by now."

"Sure, whatever, Annie. Hey Michael. Good luck keeping your wife in check. She has some bite to her."

The groom smiled. "That's one of the reasons why I married her."

- - -

"And so, in conclusion, I would just like to say cheers to the newlywed couple. May the two of you find eternal happiness in each other's company," Ryan said, raising his glass to the couple beside him. Cheers and whistles temporarily deafened Megan as she raised her glass to join in the toast.

"Well, I must say Ryan," Michael started as soon as he could be heard. "On behalf of Annie and myself, thank you for that wonderful, and thankfully not overly embarrassing, speech. But enough of me talking or any other speeches for now. I feel like dancing." With that, music filled the hall as the groom led his wife to the main dance floor for the first dance.

As Megan settled back into her seat to watch the couple on the floor, Ryan glanced over to his dinner date and found her smiling, a dreamy and faraway look on her face. Ryan grinned, allowing himself to relax and just look at her for a few moments. 'She looks wonderful tonight,' Ryan thought. He took in the lovely dress she wore, noting the beaded straps and the lavender color that gradually darkened to a rich purple around her ankles. At her throat hung the same rose pendant he had seen her wear earlier that week. Her black hair fell just past her shoulders and framed her face; he found himself resisting the strong urge to touch her hair for now, turning his attention to study her face. She didn't wear a lot of make-up in general and tonight was no exception. Her cheeks were naturally flushed from all the laughing she had done tonight, and the light lip-gloss she wore only helped brighten that beautiful smile of hers that seemed to be imprinted on her face. But what held him mesmerized were her eyes. Rich and dark brown in color, her eyes were now twinkling with happiness and laughter as she watched Michael and Annie give a mocking bow to the crowd as the first dance finished.

Megan finally remembered where she was and turned her head to look at Ryan, startling a little when she noticed him looking intently at her. "What?"

His smile grew. "Did I mention how lovely you look tonight?"

Meg blushed, embarrassed with the compliment. "No, you haven't…" she said and tried to look away.

Before he knew what he was doing, he reached out a hand and caught the tip of her chin to keep her from turning her head completely away. "You do,

Meg. Thanks for coming tonight." With that, he took her hand in his and brought it to his lips, kissing it lightly.

Her breath caught in her throat, half from the electricity she felt jolt through her when she felt his lips on her skin and half from the intensity of the blueness in his eyes as he watched her emotions play out on her face. "Thank you for inviting me," she found herself replying, her heart beating erratically in her chest.

"Go, Ryan! I see you've finally gotten down to business and started charming the lady," a voice laughed, interrupting the intimate moment the two were sharing.

"What? And let the opportunity pass me by? I think not," Ryan laughed back. "So are you two done with the dance floor yet or must we go on watching you two have all the fun?"

"Well, we're not through dancing yet but we were just wondering if you guys were ever going to join."

"I was just about to ask," he smiled and the newlywed couple moved on to encourage another couple to join them on the dance floor. "So what do you say? Ready to dance?"

"Of course," she said, allowing herself to be pulled to her feet.

- - -

"So Ryan, I thought you said you were leaving by the end of the week and you're still here. What gives?"

He laughed as he and Megan twirled around on the dance floor. "Technically, it's not the end of the week yet. I stayed for the wedding and was planning on heading out afterwards."

"I see. Do you have rehearsals or something to do for the upcoming tour? You guys start that in a couple weeks, don't you?"

"Ahh, so you are a fan. Not one of those crazy stalker types, right?"

"I can promise you no. I just like your music."

"Glad to hear," he nodded. "And no, I wasn't leaving because of the tour, at least not exactly. That's just when my ticket said I was leaving," he laughed.

"Oh god, I must sound like such a dork right now. I'm sorry. I just assumed-"

"No, don't worry about it, Meg. Really. You're not a dork."

"That just shows how little you know," she laughed. "Anyway, so you leave tonight?"

"I don't know."

"You just said your ticket was for tonight."

"I did," he smiled.

"Then…"

"I don't know if I want to leave just yet." He smiled at her confused look. "I'd like to stay, if…" He hesitated, suddenly unsure of himself.

"If what Ryan?" she asked, intrigued by the sudden shy feeling she was getting from him.

'Ry, you might as well go for it and see how she reacts. You've felt comfortable with her thus far and there's no denying the spark that was there just kissing her on the hand. Something big is here right in front of you.' He took a breath. "I'll stay if you can give me a reason to stay."

Megan felt a wave of emotions wash through her. 'He did not just say what I think he said, did he?' But he had, and he was still looking at her, an anxious expression on his face that she was unfamiliar with as he awaited her answer. She smiled. "I'd love it if you stayed, Ryan." 'Oh my god, did I just say that? To 'the' Ryan Garner? What is the world coming to,' she asked herself, wondering why she was letting her emotions rule her all of a sudden. 'I mean true, it was an honest answer...'

He gave a small smile and kissed her on the forehead before gathering her closer in his arms, letting her rest her head on his chest as they swayed to the slow music, giving them both time to think through what had just passed between the two. "Thank you," he whispered. As Megan unconsciously snuggled her head against his chest some more, Ryan held her that much tighter, recognizing that they were both dealing with some intense emotions right now. 'So what's up, Ry? It's just not like you to be this way. You've got to think. There's a brutal media out there that's ready to ruin everything we've worked so hard to gain so far. You can't afford any bad press right now, not when we're about to start up our next tour. You've got to be more careful!' But he couldn't reprimand himself for too long. All he could think about was how good it felt to have Megan in his arms. 'I know there's no rule or law saying I can't see other people while I'm in the band, but can I put her through that? She's like no one else. There's just something about her that makes me feel like this is all right. No one has ever come close to that before. I wonder why...'

Ryan felt a slight tap on his shoulder and he pulled away slightly from Megan. She blinked open her eyes and found a man whispering into Ryan's ear. He nodded and the man went away. He turned back to his date and saw her questioning him with his eyes. He took his time answering though, an idea forming in his head... "Hey, did you see the latest movie with Paul Jumper and Caitlyn Zephyr?"

"The one that came out last month? Yeah, I did. What kind of question is that?"

"Do you remember the theme song?"

She thought for a moment. "It had something to do with lifetime and love, right? Is that it?"

A brilliant smile lit up his face. "That's the one. Come with me." With that, he led her off the dance floor and over to the area set up for the DJ. He handed her a microphone. "Do you remember the words?"

Realization finally hit her and she started to protest once the microphone was in her hands. "Ryan! There is no way I'm singing in front of all these people just like that!"

"You won't be alone. I'll be singing with you. Part of my duties tonight is to help provide some entertainment with a couple songs. You'll only be helping me out in one of them. I just thought it'd be a nice treat for the audience to hear some variety and not just me singing."

"But I haven't even warmed up. My voice sucks right now since it's summer and I haven't really sung since spring."

"Excuses, Meg. Just think of this as a karaoke bar."

"I don't do karaoke," she glowered at him. "I hate karaoke."

"Please?" He took her hand in his and held it to his heart. "Please," he asked again.

Her sharp retort died in her throat when she found herself melting underneath that intense blue gaze of his and she could feel the warmth spreading from his chest going into her hand. Sighing, she gave up. "You owe me, Ryan. Which parts do you want me to sing?"

The two reviewed the sheet music for a minute while the DJ got ready behind them. Soon, though, the opening chords were being played and Ryan took another microphone. "Ladies and gentlemen, I'd like Michael and Annie to take the dance floor to themselves again for this next song." As the crowd dispersed and the newlyweds found themselves in the spotlight again, Ryan continued. " Annie, Michael, we dedicate this song to you."

With that, the opening chords finished and the cue was given. Ryan started to sing.

Follow the stars, our guiding light - they cannot lead us astray.

Megan couldn't believe she was doing this but she couldn't back out now. Megan took in a deep breath.

This is the moment to take our chance and rise up for the

light!

For a moment, she found herself at the center of attention when she began to sing. She saw Annie give her a smile of encouragement before being drawn closer in Michael's arms for the slow dance. Next to her, Ryan took her hand in his and squeezed it gently for support as well before he joined in to harmonize with her.

Going through my days loving you is all my heart could ever do.

Megan turned her attention away from the dance floor to look at Ryan and found him already looking at her. Again, she felt him squeeze her hand and smiled, finally allowing herself to relax and just sing her heart out.

Others have their stories. We will rise and fall, too.
Yet rise again, together, stronger than ever before.
We will have our glory as we dance through life as one.
In joy and pain, worlds will move by the strength of our love alone.

Going through my days loving you is all my heart could ever do.

Nothing else can see us through
As long as we share and save the love, come what may.
For love is worth everything after all.

Going through my days loving you is all my heart could

ever do.
Generations to come will know of our love
For this lifetime of loving you will eclipse all others.

Applause broke out for the duet, reminding Megan of where she was. "Thanks for singing, Meg," she heard Ryan whispering into her ear after a quick kiss on the cheek. "Wait for me afterward?"

"Of course," she answered, finally able to pull herself away as the DJ started up another tune to follow.

It was a slow walk back to the table as guests stopped to praise her. Once able to take a seat, she took a sip of some water and sat back to listen to Ryan sing. Before she was able to sit for very long though, she felt another presence take a seat next to her. "Good job out there, Meg."

She whipped her head around. "Ben! What are you doing here?" She reached over to give him a hug.

"I'd ask the same thing of you. Me and a couple of the guys were hired to help with the catering tonight. You know, side job and all. I didn't know you were going to sing."

"I wasn't planning on it."

"Then how come you're here?"

"I was invited."

"Really? I wouldn't think you'd know anyone in this crowd."

"I don't actually."

"Then how…"

"The guy I was singing with asked me to come tonight."

Ben turned to take a closer look at the singer right now. "He looks familiar. Do I know him from somewhere?"

"He's–"

"Hey, Megan! Great job out there!"

"Thanks, Aaron. Hey guys," she replied as another of Ben's friends pulled up some chairs to sit near them. "It's nice to see you all outside of school. What's going on?"

- - -

After his last song, Ryan waited for the applause to finish before heading off the music platform for the moment. His eyes scanned the reception hall and found Megan sitting at their dinner table. He also noticed she wasn't alone. He drew closer and found that she was surrounded by a handful of guys. He took special note of the one sitting right beside her; his arm was draped casually across Meg's shoulders and she was making no attempt to move. An unfamiliar fire burned through him and it took him a moment to realize that he was actually jealous. "Hey, Meg," he greeted her, forcibly calming himself down before he made any rash conclusions.

She reached out a hand and drew him closer, beckoning for him to sit. "Hey, Ryan. Guys, this is Ryan. Ryan, these are guys I know from college, David, Aaron, Greg, and Ben."

They all exchanged brief greetings before Ryan tugged on Megan's hand. "Feel like dancing some more?"

"Sure. I'll see the rest of you later, all right?"

When her friends agreed, he successfully pulled Megan away from under Ben's arm and brought her back onto the dance floor. With his jealous side subsided for now, Ryan smiled down at Megan. "What did I tell you? You have a great singing voice."

She shrugged. "You made a lucky guess."

"That wasn't luck. Luck was getting the chance to sit next to you at the theater last week. Luck is having you in my arms right now."

"Flirt," she smiled.

"I mean it." He took a hand and tipped her head up, even though they were already looking into each other's eyes. "Meg, I want you to know that I consider myself to be very lucky to have met you. I consider myself lucky in that I have been able to spend this much time with you."

"Ryan, that's a lot to be thankful for in such little time," she said slowly. "For all you know, I could be putting on a show for you."

"Are you?" He caught her with a pointed look.

"No, I'm not," she shook her head. "I couldn't do that."

He nodded. "I know."

She looked at him. "How?"

He shrugged. "I just do. Being in this business and being in the spotlight so much means learning how to read people quicker than most, see who to trust and who not to." They let the subject drop for a moment to just dance for a bit. "You're not like other girls, you know that, right?" He started again a few minutes later.

"What do you mean?"

"I'm not getting the feeling you're putting on any airs in front of me."

She nodded. "I'm not."

"Why?"

Meg shrugged. "That's just not me. What isn't me is me being this forward with people I've just met."

He smiled. "I can't picture you as a shy type."

"It's there. You'll just have to backtrack a little and find that part of me out somehow."

"Nah. I like you as you are now. There's no need to change something that's already perfect."

Megan laughed. "You really do know how to make a girl feel special, don't you?"

He nodded, smiling along with her. "I try my best."

- - -

"It looks like you've found yourself a keeper, Ryan. She doesn't seem to be going after you like others."

Ryan turned and found Annie smiling up at him. Megan had gone to the restroom while Ryan went searching for their coats in order to head out. "Yet Annie. There's still time."

"No… I don't think you'll have to worry about her too much. Call it an instinct or something. Anyway, you take care of her, all right? Or I promise I will get on your case."

"I promise, Annie. You take care of yourself too, okay? Have fun on your honeymoon."

"Thanks, Ryan. And break a leg in a couple weeks if I don't get to hear from you before we get back."

Megan joined the two then and reached over to give Annie a hug. "Congratulations again on your wedding."

"Thanks sweetie. You take care now, okay?"

"I will if you will. Bye Annie. Bye Michael."

Michael waved good-bye to Megan and Ryan as the two joined a group of people leaving. Outside, Charles stood near the entrance, waiting for them. He led them back to the car and began the drive back to Megan's house. There, Ryan walked her to the door. "Thanks for coming again," he said.

"Thank you for inviting me. I had a lot of fun tonight."

"I'm glad." An awkward silence followed, neither of them wanting the night to end. "So... Can I call you?"

Megan laughed. "Of course, Ryan. Here," she tore out a piece of paper from a notepad she kept in her purse for notes and jotted it down. "Good night, Ryan," she said, stepping up onto her tiptoes to give him a kiss on the cheek.

"Good night, Megan. Sweet dreams."

Megan smiled and finally forced herself into the house. With heavy steps, Ryan walked the way back down the driveway and into the car. As the two drove away, back toward the city, Charles asked, "Good night, sir?"

Ryan paused for a moment, reliving a few moments from the night. "No, Charles," he replied. "It was a great night," he finished, clutching the piece of paper in his hand.

7 | Part of Your World

"Good morning, sleepy head," Megan grinned as Lori stumbled into the kitchen, rubbing her eyes in hopes of waking up.

"God, Meg, I don't get you sometimes. You come home late and you're still up before me. How do you do it?"

"Internal clock, remember? So do you want anything?" she asked, getting up. "Bagel? Toast? Cereal? Coffee?"

"Just some juice if you have any," Lori answered, plopping herself down in a chair and yawning loudly. "Thanks," she replied when the glass was placed in front of her.

"You're welcome. So how was yesterday for you?"

"Other than quiet and a little lonely?"

"Sorry! You're the one who told me to go!"

"I know, Meg. I'm just kidding. And I'm glad you went. I got some stuff that needed to be done finished."

"Well that's good."

"Yup. Last night was productive until I saw a certain tape in your collection." She grinned. "Do you remember the musical we were in?"

"Oh god, you watched that while I was gone?" she laughed.

"Hey, it brought back some good memories."

"Sure, if you don't remember all the stress we were in, taking tests and such. Wait, I'm still doing that."

Lori laughed. "That's your fault for deciding to go into medicine and being crazy enough to take summer classes on top of your internships."

"And I'm still hoping that it will all be worth it in the end."

"It will be, Meg. I've seen how passionate you are about this. You'll be fine."

"I hope so."

"I know so."

Meg laughed. "So what do you feel like doing today?"

"First, I want to hear about yesterday."

Meg smiled. "All right, so it was better than good. It was almost…" She paused, searching her mind for the appropriate word. "Magical is as close to what I felt as I can describe. There was almost a fairytale like feeling."

Lori grinned. "It sure sounds like he's charmed you. Do I hear any wedding bells for you anytime soon?"

Megan burst out laughing out loud before quieting down just as quickly when she realized her other roommates were probably still asleep. "Lori, you know that this was technically only the second time we've seen each other. I hardly deem that as long enough to get to know each other well enough, let alone tie the knot together."

"Well, you know there are people out there who get married after only knowing each other for a week, sometimes even less."

M. A. Valdellon

"True, but I'm not one of those people. You know how careful and picky I am in choosing my friends. Why should marriage be any different?"

"You've got me there, Meg." Lori looked at her best friend sitting next to her at the table. It seemed as if something was different about her. The sparkle in her eyes and the smile on her face... It had been a long time since she'd seen her this happy before. Lori smiled. "So when are you going to talk to him again?"

Meg shrugged. "He's going to call me."

"When?"

"I don't know. All I know is that this is in his hands now."

"Right... And if he's a typical guy, he won't call for the next couple of days."

"If it happens, then it happens. I'm not going to just sit around and wait for his call, and I'm not going to make the next move if I don't have to."

"Why not? You like him!"

She nodded. "But I'm also biased in a way. How do I know for sure how he feels about me? He could have still been sweet talking me the entire time."

"Do you believe that?"

"Not really," she admitted. "But I don't want to get my hopes up either. He's Ryan Garner! Hot, cute, and famous guy here. What are my chances with someone like him?"

"Meg," she groaned. "Let's not go through this again, please?"

She smiled. "Fine. Now what do you want to do today?"

"Well, I had nothing special in mind. Why don't

70

we just go hit the mall or something? We can get some shopping done while you give me the details about yesterday. Maybe we can even hit a movie."

Meg nodded, getting up to put their dishes away in the sink. "Then let's get going."

- - -

"You actually sang with him!?" Lori screeched, drawing the attention of a few neighboring shoppers as the two looked through the racks of a department store.

"Hush, Lori! You don't have to announce it to the whole world. But anyway, yes. I sang with him just like that."

Lori looked at Meg with a look of surprise on her face. Then she shook her head and smiled. "You better watch yourself Meg. Not only has he got you smitten but he's already getting you to do favors for him as well. Before you know it, you'll be throwing yourself down at his feet just to please him."

"As if I would ever let myself stoop down to that level, literally or not," she retorted. "I do have a sense of pride and self-worth too, you know."

Lori laughed. "I know. But I just wanted to see the expression on your face."

Meg rolled her eyes. "You are just too much sometimes," she said as she moved onto the next rack.

"But you know you love it."

"I do, and I miss it when you're gone."

"I know. I miss it too. That's why you have to come back east sometime. Vacations aren't enough anymore."

"They never were enough, Lori, but I guess you're right. As soon as all these tests are done and whenever I get leave from the clinic, I'll try to go over. I suppose it is my turn since you're here now."

"Uh huh. And I've already got a few new places to show you when you do get around to coming."

Meg smiled. "The fun never ends, does it?"

"Not with us," she smiled back.

"Anyway, have you found anything you like?"

"Just these," Lori answered, holding up a couple of tops. "I want to try them on first though."

"All right. I think the dressing rooms are over there," Meg pointed as she started leading the way.

As Meg waited for Lori to come out so she could help judge how the blouses fit her, her cell phone rang. "Hello?"

"Hello, Meg?"

Megan felt a grin spread across her face. "Yup, it's me. How'd you get this number, Ryan?"

"I called your house number and one of your roommates told me to try your cell."

"You're lucky I actually turned it on today. I usually forget to."

She felt a warm feeling spread through her body as Ryan's deep laughter rang in her ears. "I know. Your roommate warned me about that possibility."

Meg answered with a laugh of her own. "So what's up?"

"Nothing much. I was just wondering what you were doing today."

"Well, I'm actually shopping and hanging out with one of my best friends today."

"Oh…"

Meg smiled, hearing the disappointment in his voice. "What are you doing today?"

"Well, since I hadn't actually planned on staying past last night, I really have nothing to do now."

"Well then, why don't you join us? We really didn't have anything set to do either other than shop and maybe see a movie."

"Oh no, Meg. I don't want to impose on you."

Meg laughed. "You won't be, trust me."

"Are you sure?"

"Yes, I'm sure."

"Well, if you insist…"

"I do. Besides, I don't want you to be spending all this time by yourself if I can help it."

"Aww, thank you, Meg."

"You're welcome. I just hope you're okay with the shopping and stuff."

"Hey, if it means spending time getting to know you and your friends, I'm all for it."

Meg felt warmth touch her heart and it was her turn to say thank you. "So how do you want us to meet? Should I pick you up or do you have a way of getting here?"

"Well, Charles actually left already and I haven't had the chance to actually rent a car yet so…"

"Say no more. We'll be there in a bit. Are you still at the same hotel?"

"Yeah, but I'm also thinking about checking out too."

Meg felt her heart drop. "Why?"

"Because I was wondering if there was something closer to where you live. I don't want either of us to waste the time and money needed to travel back and forth."

"I see your point. Yeah, why don't you go ahead and get your things packed and check out if you like. I know of a place downtown here. We can move you in and then go back out to eat lunch and stuff."

"Sounds good to me."

"Okay. I'll let Lori know and we'll be on our way. I'll call you when we get close to the hotel, all right?"

"Sure. I'll see you in a little bit."

"Bye." Meg looked up to find Lori looking back at her. She grinned.

"Who were you talking to just now?"

Instead of answering, she began to lead the way out towards the parking lot after noticing that her friend's hands were empty. "Didn't fit?"

"Nope."

"All right. We'll find something later on I'm sure. Right now, we have to go to the city."

"What for?"

"We're picking someone up."

"Who-" Lori stopped and took note of the goofy grin on Meg's face and found herself smiling back. "Does he mind me being around?"

"Not at all. He was more worried about you minding his presence actually."

"As if I would really mind something like that."

"My words exactly. I just hope you don't mind eating a late lunch."

"What's lunch when I get the chance to meet the guy who's swept one of my best friends off her feet?"

Megan laughed as the two exited the store and walked out into the sunshine.

- - -

"Please, Lori? My hands are full here driving."

"Fine." Lori took Meg's cell phone into her hand and dialed the number.

The phone picked up after the first ring. "Hello. Megan?"

"No. This is Lori. Meg's driving but we wanted to let you know that we're almost there. A couple minutes max."

"All right. I'll head outside then."

"Okay. See you in a few."

"Bye."

She hung up the phone. "Thanks, Lori," Meg said.

"No problem."

A minute later, the two were pulling up to the curb in front of the hotel and stopping pretty close to where Ryan was waiting with his one suitcase. "Is that all you brought with you?" Meg asked as she got out and walked to the back to help him load it into the trunk.

"Yup, this is it. I didn't need a lot considering I'd planned on this being a relatively short trip."

"If you say so," she grinned. "So how are you?" she asked as she slammed the trunk shut and began turning to go back to the driver's side.

"Better now that you're around," he answered, stalling her by slipping an arm around her waist and kissing her lightly on the cheek.

"What was that for?" she asked when he let go of her. She could still feel the warmth of his body linger on her as she grabbed his hand and led him to her side of the car. His open display of affection had caught her off guard and her insides were feeling all mushy.

"Just my way of saying hello."

Meg smiled. "Well thank you. Hello to you, too," she laughed as they both climbed into the car. "Anyway, Ryan, this is one of my best friends Lori. Lori, meet Ryan." The two said their respective hellos as Meg pulled back out into the traffic. "So where do you guys want to go? Do you want to eat lunch first or should we go to the hotel and check you in, Ryan?"

"Honestly, I don't care," he answered.

"Lori?"

"Why don't we just grab some fast food on the way? I didn't really eat anything for breakfast this morning."

"Fast food it is. We can have dinner somewhere better later."

After receiving no objections, Meg continued to drive their way out of the city and begin the trip back to the college town.

- - -

"So wait," Ryan was saying as he sat back in his seat. He'd eaten his share of food pretty quickly and was now waiting for the other two to finish their meals. "Didn't you say something last week about being in school?"

Meg groaned. "Must you remind me? I'm going to pay dearly later for hardly studying this past week."

"Relax. You've got a week until your next exam," Lori said, trying to help. "You can make it up."

"Lori, you're a doll and everything but you just don't realize how tough these upper division science exams can be. Especially for this professor! I hear that it's already nearly impossible trying to pass the class let alone doing well enough to get an A."

"And how many times has what you heard about a class been actually true? You know former students usually try to psych the younger ones out."

Meg laughed. "That is true, but I'm still not going to take any chance."

"You worry too much, you know that?" Lori laughed.

Meg nodded. "Usually with good reason though."

Ryan smiled. Seeing Meg this relaxed was definitely a good thing, he thought. Last night, he'd felt that she'd still held back. He understood though. In the company of strangers, he was typically reserved as well. But the glimpses he'd seen of her true personality then and at the theater and especially now with her best friend around were well worth waiting for. "Maybe I shouldn't stay then," he found himself saying. "I don't want to jeopardize your grade by distracting you."

Immediately, she turned her attention back to him and brushed him off. "Don't worry about it. You're here to enjoy yourself and I'll be there to make sure you do."

He grinned. "Is that a threat?"

She nodded, grinning back. "Besides, it will be the ultimate challenge for me to see if I can use all the time management skills I've learned over the years."

"With Ryan around? Yeah right! You have yet to apply that policy whenever there's a cute guy around," Lori supplied.

"Lori!" Meg shrieked, blushing furiously as Ryan and Lori laughed at her. "That's not true!" Her friend couldn't answer; she was just laughing too hard at the look on Meg's face.

Ryan felt himself relax more at the sight. 'She's not hiding from me. She's not holding back now, I can feel it,' he thought to himself as the three finally got up to hit the road again. 'I can learn to like this. Oh what are you saying Ry? You know you love it already. It's been a while since you didn't have to worry about saving face and such in the public. Besides the times when I'm with guys or the people at home, I can't relax so much. With Meg...' He looked at her and smiled to himself. 'She treats me like a normal person even though she knew pretty much straight off the bat who I am. That means a lot. I wonder if she knows how much I appreciate that. How can I thank her enough for letting me be a part of her world? Even if it is only for a couple more days until I really have to leave, it'll still be a big deal to me.' But in his heart, he hoped that this would last for more than a few days and that Meg felt the same way about this too.

8 | Hi-Ho! Hi-Ho!

"Good morning," Meg greeted as she stood on her tiptoes to give Ryan a quick kiss on the cheek. "How was your night?" she asked after he had locked his door and they began to make their way to her car.

"It was all right. I slept well."

"That's great."

"Yeah. How about you? Did Lori leave okay?"

Meg thought back to the night before and grinned. She recalled how she and her best friend had talked the entire time she'd driven Lori to the airport.

"I can't believe it!" Lori exclaimed.

"Believe what?"

"You're finally dating someone! And not just anyone. You're going out with Ryan Garner! How often can I say I know someone who's dating a real, live pop star?"

Meg laughed. "Come on, Lori. You know it's nothing really serious. We're just hanging out."

"Keep telling yourself that and maybe you'll believe that one. Yesterday, you and Ryan couldn't keep your lovey dovey eyes off each other."

"Oh please. Your imagination is running away with you again."

"That's what you think. I'm just upset that I have to leave before he does. Then again, maybe it's a good thing

I am going. Now the two of you can have some private time to yourselves to really get to know each other."

"There's no rush, Lori. He's just another guy."

"Right, Meg. He's just an ordinary guy who just happens to be part of Pulse, literally the hottest group right now."

"You know I don't focus on that."

"I know, but you both will have to talk about it sometime. He's not staying here forever, and it'll be better to talk about this sooner than later." She sighed. "There's a lot of chemistry between you two, Meg. I've seen it, meaning I know that at least you've felt it. I just hope things will work out for you guys."

"What do you mean?" she asked, glancing over to her friend. "Why wouldn't it work out?"

"Besides the whole long distance thing?"

"What of it? I've seen you and Tony do it. You've been together for so many years now and the two of you still love and trust each other."

"But this isn't about us or any other couple. This is about you and Ryan, Meg. Think about it. How many solid relationships have you been in? Not many. Why? Because you won't let anything or anyone get in the way of your dreams of going into medicine. You've put so much time and effort to get where you are today and I don't see you throwing it all away for nothing.

"At the same time, there's Ryan," she continued. "He's living a fantasy right now, doing something he loves to do, which is entertaining people all around the world. He's not going to give that up."

"And I'm not going to ask him to give anything up either, Lori. I think I'd hate myself too much if I was responsible for doing that to him."

Lori nodded. "I know but I'm just warning you it's going to be a tough road ahead now that you're together."

"But we're not–"

"You will be, Meg," she cut her off. "The two of you like each other enough and I can see you both putting in the time and effort to make it work."

"So what's the problem?"

Again, Lori sighed. "Finding a balance. The two of you have your lives set right now. You know what you want and how to get there. He does too. But to rework each other's lives to fit the other into that plan somehow? Soon, you'll be making sacrifices to keep the relationship going. Given, that comes in any relationship, but I think his fame will make this harder than anyone of us can realize."

Meg nodded. "I know that, Lori. I've already thought about that and more. Why do you think I haven't dated much? It's not only because I don't have the time or found the right person or whatever, but I also know that relationships can be distractions if they're not the right one. That's why nothing's going to happen between Ryan and myself, at least not now."

"But you like him, right?"

Meg nodded her head. "I do like him, but liking someone isn't enough of a reason for me to just give it all up. I know it will be hard if and when we do decide to try something together but I don't want to force myself to try to get into something with him when I don't think it'd be fair to either of us if I still have hesitations over the whole ordeal."

"Fair enough," Lori said. "It's a good thing that rational side of your mind still works."

"And the day it stops working, I'll be sure that you or Ben or Ken or anyone else will be right there to make sure that it's beaten back into me."

The two laugh as Meg pulled up to the curb. "Thanks for driving me, Meg," Lori said as she took a suitcase out of the trunk.

"Any time, Lori. Are you sure you don't want company?"

"I'm sure. You go on home and keep Ryan company while you study."

"All right, will do. You take care and call me when you're back home."

"Of course. Just keep me up to date with all the details on everything."

Meg grinned. "I will, knowing that if I didn't, you'll personally hunt me down somehow."

"Of course," Lori smiled.

The two hugged. "Thanks for coming, Lori."

"I'll see you soon."

And with that, the two parted, Lori heading into the airport while Meg walked back to her car to go back home.

"Yeah, Lori left all right. I got a call from her already letting me know she's back at home," Meg found herself saying.

"That's good."

"Uh huh. Anyway, did you eat yet?"

"Are you kidding? I just woke up fifteen minutes ago."

Meg laughed. "I wouldn't know. All right. Let's get you fed before I sit you in the waiting room for the morning."

- - -

Half an hour later, Meg was still hovering by Ryan's side. "Now, are you sure you want to stay here? Once I go back there, I won't be able to talk to you until my shift is through."

"I'll be fine, Meg. Don't worry about me."

"I can't help it. This is your last day here and you're going to waste half of it sitting here by yourself. You're going to lose even more time afterward because I still have to go to class in the afternoon."

Ryan laughed. "Stop it, Meg. I'm here because I want to be here. Just go do your thing. I'll be fine," he firmly stated, even as he pulled his beanie down further on his head and put on a pair of glasses in an attempt to hide who he was.

"Fine. I'll go. But I'm telling you that if you need to get out and go, just go. There's nothing holding you here. Just be back by noon so we can leave."

"I'll keep it in mind if and when I decide I'm too bored with watching the television or reading some magazines. I've even got a pen and some paper with me so I can work on some stuff. Or I could play some video games," he said, pointing to the video game console located in one corner of the room.

"Go right ahead and watch TV or read or work but the video games are off limits for you. You're not a patient," she said, grinning a little.

He shrugged and smiled back. "It was worth a shot. I'll see you in a while, okay?"

"Sure." And with that, Meg turned around and

walked through a door to begin preparing for the morning's clinic.

She went to each of the patient rooms, unlocking each and making sure that everything was in place. Then she checked to make sure they were all stocked with the necessary supplies for the doctors to use. After that, she went to the nurse's station to check on the number of patients coming in this morning. She sighed upon seeing that there were close to fifteen patients in both the cardiology and the hematology clinics this morning. She looked up at the limited number of rooms they had and groaned inwardly. Overlapping patients were always a problem and there was no doubt that she and Ben were going to be tired by the time lunch came around and they were set free. 'What a way to start a Monday,' she thought to herself as she glanced at the clock and saw that there were five minutes before the clinic opened. She went up front to help Connie finish setting up in the receptionist's area. Besides, it let her peek and see what Ryan was up to. 'Not like that's a bad thing,' she rationalized. 'Technically, clinic hasn't opened yet. Just as long as I don't find myself wandering over here too much once we get to work... I'm sure that once the patients start coming in, I won't have any time anyway.'

- - -

"Meg? Little Vicky needs to have her blood pressure retaken."

"Sure thing, Dr. Keen. Room fifteen, right?" She

saw her supervisor nod her head before moving on to the back conference room to write down some notes for her report on the patient. Megan walked into the patient's room and found herself smiling. "Hey Vicky! How are you this morning?" she asked as she came closer to the baby and leaned down to tickle her a little, earning a giggle as the child clapped its chubby hands together. "She's gotten so big now, Mrs. Holstein."

"That she has. She's getting to be quite a handful."

"I can imagine so. Would you mind picking her up? I need to get the cuff around her foot because her arm is still too small to take her blood pressure there."

"No problem." The mother waited patiently as Megan did her task and started to take the baby's child pressure. "So how are you, Meg? It's been a few weeks since I've seen you."

"Because Vicky's been getting healthier and doesn't need to come by for check ups so often, I notice," she smiled. "Things are good. You know, the usual school and stuff."

"That's good. I assume you're doing well as always. Is Dr. Keen treating you all right?"

"Of course. Strict as she is, she's a great person to intern for."

"Good. Now, are there any new guys to report to me about?"

Meg laughed. "Only you would ask me something like that."

"Well I'm just wondering. I know it's been awhile since I remember you going out for fun."

"What are you talking about? There's Ben!" she protested after telling the young mother to keep the baby still for a minute.

"Ben doesn't count. I know the two of you are more friends than anything else."

"That's true," she agreed. "But anyway, yes. There may be someone out there."

"I thought so. A nice girl like you shouldn't be alone so much."

"Maybe I shouldn't, but it's not like I have the time for such a commitment either."

"I suppose so. Anyway, what's the boy's name?"

"Ryan. You may have seen him actually."

"Really?"

Meg nodded as she wrote down the baby's child pressure on a scrap of paper to give to Dr. Keen. "Yeah, he's actually out in the waiting room."

"You dragged him to work? Megan!" the woman laughed.

"He insisted. He's here on vacation and didn't want to be alone."

"If you say so, but I still don't know… I mean, mixing work with pleasure?"

"I'm strictly on duty right now, Mrs. Holstein. You know that."

"I know, I know. I'm just teasing you," Mrs. Holstein laughed, and with that, Megan left the room to hand the paper to the doctor.

Once she was done with that task, she checked in at the nurse's station and saw that there weren't any charts out, meaning that there were no new patients to check in just yet. She welcomed this little break and found herself looking at Ben, who was also sitting there, lounging around. "No one?"

"Nope. About time too. If we get another person, we'll be overbooked on rooms."

"As if that would be our biggest worry in the clinic," she grinned.

"That's true. So what's new? I see that Ryan's out there."

"You noticed?" He nodded. "Did you say hi?"

"Nah. I didn't get a chance to since I got in a little late."

"I was wondering what happened to you."

"Slept in," he grinned.

"You're so bad. Did Dr. Keen notice?"

"Nope, and don't tell her either." She laughed. "So really. What's new? This is the second time I've seen him around you in the past week. Something's going on."

"No, there isn't."

"Come on, Meg. It's been a long time since you've dated anyone seriously, and that was me a while ago. Are you holding out?"

"As if I would ever hide something from you, Ben."

"Well don't start now. What's up?"

"I told you. Nothing really. We're just hanging out."

"Please. You always say that."

"I do not," she started to whine but was interrupted.

"Ben! Meg! New patients!"

The two jumped up onto their feet and grabbed the new charts from Connie. Quickly, the two set to work, going through the records to make a note on what these new children needed in terms of care that morning. Meg finished first and went to the door. "Leslie?" She stole a quick glance to Ryan as she waited for her patient and her parents to come forward and noticed him smiling back at her, his face half hidden by a magazine. She smiled before stepping aside to let the small family through and leading them down the hall to another room. There, she had the little girl sit down and remove her shoes while she took her temperature. "Has she had this fever for long?" she asked the parents before leading the child over to the scale to weigh her.

"Well she started feeling sick yesterday afternoon."

"Has she taken any medication for it?"

"Just a little Tylenol last night and this morning before we got here."

"All right," she said, making a note of it on the chart. "Leslie? Can you get off the scale and stand by that ruler now? I'd like to see how much you've grown since you've last been here," she said. Once that was done, Meg told the little girl to put on her shoes again before leading the three into another room. She heard Ben call out for his patient after they left the room and smiled. "Dr. Keen will be with you in a few minutes," she said after turning on the light in the room.

Then she went back to the conference room to put the new chart in for the doctor and signed the new patient in on the time sheet. With that done, she went back to check on the other rooms. She saw Mrs. Holstein packing her things up and waited patiently for her to leave before going in and straightening up the room after her. "Take care, Mrs. Holstein."

"I will. It was nice seeing you again, Meg," the woman said as she walked to the receptionist area to schedule Vicky's next appointment.

- - -

It was already half past noon by the time Meg walked back out into the waiting room and found Ryan sitting in the same chair he'd been in all morning. "Sorry about that. That last patient came in a little late."

"No problem, I understand."

She nodded. "Ready to head out?"

"But of course."

"All right." She waved good-bye to Connie and led Ryan out into the hallway to the elevators. "How was your morning?"

"It was all right. I got some work done. What about you? You looked busy in there."

"Eh. It wasn't too bad. It was just another normal day. Now come on. Let's get some lunch," she said as the elevator doors opened and they stepped in.

9 | Second Star to the Right

Ryan looked at Megan as she drove them towards the city where he'd finally be catching a flight back home. He had turned slightly in his seat so he could study her profile. After her work at the clinic, they'd gone back to her house so she could change into clothes more suitable for the heat. Now, she was dressed casually in a T-shirt, a pair of jean shorts, and some flip-flops. Her long, black hair was up in a messy ponytail. He found himself reaching over to gently tuck some hair behind her ear. Her hair was soft to his touch and he let his hand trail down her neck lightly. Soft, late afternoon light filtered into the car, adding to the beauty that he knew to already radiated from inside her as she smiled and leaned into his touch a little.

"You better stop that, Ryan. You're distracting me from my driving and I don't want to get into an accident here."

"Sorry," he apologized, smiling and pulling his hand away. He wasn't really sorry though. He knew that she enjoyed it, probably nearly as much as he liked touching her. For him, touching her was a physical reminder that she was really there and that this wasn't all a dream. 'At the same time, she's definitely her own person,' he thought to himself as he remembered how he had asked her what she'd wanted for her birthday earlier.

"What are you talking about? You're a little too late for that now."

"So I'm off by a few days. I still want to get you something."

"Don't. I don't want anything."

"I insist, Meg."

"Really, it's okay. I'm fine with just having this chance to spend time with you."

"I'm flattered, but I still want to get you something."

"No."

"Yes."

"No!"

"Yes!"

Meg looked up at him, exasperated. "You're not going to take no for an answer now, are you?"

"Of course not. So what do you want?"

She looked at him quietly for a moment, thinking hard about what she should say. A small smile formed on her face the longer she looked at him though. In the end, she said, "I'll tell you what I don't want and you can take it from there. I don't want jewelry, I don't want flowers, and I don't want chocolates."

He looked at her aghast. "What woman doesn't want jewelry, flowers, or chocolates? I thought that was some kind of defining characteristic that helped linked all women together."

She grinned. "Not me. Jewelry and flowers just aren't my thing."

"But what about your necklace? You've worn that every time I've seen you. And it's of a rose!"

"All right, let me rephrase what I said. I don't really have a thing for real flowers. They're pretty and all for a

*while but then they wilt and die. I like things that last.
And this necklace along with the watch I'm wearing is
probably the most jewelry you'll ever see on me on most
occasions, and I wear the necklace because it's from my
parents. They got it for me on my birthday."*

*"Okay, fine. You've given me valid explanations on
why you wouldn't want jewelry or flowers. What about
chocolates?"*

*"They're not very healthy for me in large quantities,"
she had laughed.*

"Talk about déjà vu," Ryan found Megan saying
as they took the off-ramp leading to the airport. "I
think I've been here way too many times too
recently."

"And always saying good-bye," he added.

"Ugh! Don't remind me. It was depressing
enough knowing that no one could really stay for
that long to catch up and all."

"I understand," he answered.

Minutes later, the two were walking into the
airport hand in hand. They didn't talk. They didn't
need to say anything right now. They just wanted
to enjoy each other's company in silence for a few
moments. She stood by his side as they wove
through a line and ended up at the ticket counter for
him to check his suitcase in. And then they waited,
prolonging the moment as long as they could by
just standing there, ignoring the fact that he had to
leave in just under an hour.

Ryan sighed and drew Megan's petite body into
his arms, closing his eyes as he smelled her sweet
scent. He reluctantly pulled away a minute later,

drawing back to reach into his pocket. "Here Meg. I got you something."

"You shouldn't have! I can't-"

He put a finger to her mouth, effectively quieting her for the moment. "Just take it. I told you I'd get you something for your birthday."

She looked down and saw a small, white box in his hands, a thin, red ribbon tied around it. She took it into her hands and put her finger on the bow to begin untying it when Ryan's hands stopped her.

"Not yet. Open it when you're back home."

She nodded, tucking it away in her purse before stepping back into his arms to draw in his warm embrace.

A few moments of silence passed before he spoke again. "Thank you, Meg."

She drew back a little so she could look into his eyes. "For what, Ryan?" she said quietly, being mindful of speaking low to not draw unneeded attention to themselves out in the public.

"For being you. For treating me like any other normal guy."

"But that was nothing. Why shouldn't I treat you like that?"

He shrugged. "Most people forget that there's another side to me other than the public image I have to put on. They treat me differently, like I'm above them when in reality, I don't deserve it."

"But you've worked hard to make your dreams come true. If anything else, you've earned the respect people give you."

"Maybe not respect in a lot of cases, but I get what you mean. Still, I want to thank you."

She smiled. "I don't think I've earned a thanks, but you're welcome anyway."

He chuckled and kissed her forehead gently. "I'm going to miss you."

"I'll miss you too, but at least with you gone, I can finally get some studying done," she teased.

"Hey! I think I'm hurt," he grinned.

"Baby."

"But you still like me."

She nodded. "I don't know why, but yeah, I still like you."

Ryan chuckled. "Good, because I think you're growing on me too."

"Is that a good thing?"

He watched her closely as he answered. "When it's enough that I actually think that I could find myself falling in love you, if we can keep on like this," he added with a rush. "Then yeah, I'd like to think that it's a good thing."

Meg stiffened a little in his arms and pulled away to stare at him, searching his eyes. "I don't know what to say, Ryan."

Disappointment washed over him. "Well, I was hoping you'd say you feel the same way," he said slowly.

She smiled at him. "Ryan, there's no denying that I'm attracted to you, but remember, we've only really known each other for a week now. How can you say that?"

"Because I feel it. I know what I'm feeling."

"But how do I know you're not just lying to me, saving face in saying good-bye because you're going away in a few minutes and will be guaranteed to meet someone better than me when you guys get back on the road?"

He did not like the way this conversation was going. "What can I do to prove my feelings for you?" he pleaded, an anguished look on his face.

She hesitated before answering him quietly, "Just… don't lie to me."

"Sweetie, I've never lied to you before and I won't start lying to you anytime in the future, I swear this."

She nodded. "All right. I know you won't lie to me just as I know I can't lie to you. But that doesn't hide the fact that things are going so fast for us. I'm scared and worried, Ryan. I admit I have really strong feelings for you too, but I'm not sure if that's a good thing. I'm not one to really let my feelings take over like this."

Ryan gathered her close in his arms and rested his chin on her head where it lay on his chest, rocking her gently. "I know, Meg. I'm scared too. You're bringing out a side of me I didn't even know I had. You're right. Things are happening between us at too quickly of a pace. Maybe it's a good thing I'm going away after all. The time apart will let us see where we both stand and give us time to collect ourselves. But Megan," he said, drawing away from her a bit so he could look into her eyes. "That doesn't stop me from believing that I'm falling for you."

She gave a small smile, tears starting to form in the corners of her eyes. "I know, Ryan."

The two held each other close for a few more minutes. Then she felt him sigh and looked up. She followed his gaze to the departure screen and saw that it was time for him to go. She looked back up at him. "Are you going to be okay?"

"Yeah. I'll live at least. I just wish I didn't have to go."

"You have to get on with your own life now."

Ryan shrugged as he reached down in between the two to pick up his travel bags. Then he turned to start heading toward the terminal but Megan's arm on his stopped him. "What?"

She looked at him, slowly memorizing his face for comfort these next few weeks without him near. She smiled sadly and drew him close for one last hug. "I think I'm falling in love you too, Ryan. Take care of yourself and think of me," she whispered into his ear.

And just as quickly, she was gone, already walking away from him and becoming a part of the swirling crowd. His cheek burned from the kiss she'd given him right before the hug. He forced himself to turn away and head off to catch his flight but it wasn't until he was already up in the air that the full impact of what she'd said hit him and he found a grin spreading on his face. 'She's falling for me,' he thought. 'But what if she was lying?' As soon as that thought had filled his head though, he immediately suppressed it, already hearing her voice in his head reprimanding him. 'I don't lie, Ryan. You know that,' he could just hear her say. 'I know, Meg. You can't lie to me either.'

Ryan turned to look out into the sky as the plane rose higher and higher. The sun had set and the stars were just beginning to show in the quickly darkening sky. Immediately, his eyes were drawn to one star in particular.

"Look. See that star?" Ryan was asking Meg as the two looked up into the night sky.

"Which one?" she asked.

"That one," he said, directing her gaze to one particularly bright star that had managed to shine through the thin clouds that night. "The second star to the right in that open patch of sky over there."

She nodded. "I see it."

He hugged her close. "There's a story going around that when someone wishes on a star, the star hears it, and it starts shining brighter as it works on making that person's deepest wishes come true. That star up there that I pointed out? It's been shining really bright these past few days."

"And why is that?" she asked, intrigued by his tale.

"Because I wished that I could always be here to make you happy. It's worked so far."

Meg grinned as he tightened his arms around her, his hands clasped lightly over her own. He bent his head slightly down and kissed her softly on the neck before he kissed her lightly on the cheek.

Ryan sought out that star and found it soon enough. "Star light, star bright," he whispered to himself. "First star I see tonight. I wish I may, I wish I might, have the wish I wish tonight. Little star, you've been good to me so far. Please don't let me down anytime in the future. I just wish that things between Megan and I will be this perfect in the future as it has been these past few days…"

- - -

Back at home, Megan found herself in her room getting ready for bed. Just as she was about to turn out the light though, she remembered the gift Ryan had given her at the airport.

She slipped out from underneath the covers, retrieved the white box from her purse, and climbed back into bed. Finally, she undid the ribbon and lifted open the lid. Her fingers carefully pulled back the tissue paper and she gave a small gasp. Her breath caught in her throat as she lifted out a small, clay, star picture frame. Where the picture should have been was the star story he had told her in his handwriting. She smiled as she took it out of the box and turned it in the light, a small smile forming on her face.

Still clutching the small weight in her hand, she turned the light off and climbed back out of bed to go to her window. She drew aside a curtain and sought out the star Ryan had pointed out to her only the night before. "Star light, star bright," she found herself saying. "First star I see tonight. I wish I may, I wish I might, have the wish I wish tonight. Please little star. Let this past week be just the beginning of a wonderful relationship. I don't want to regret having said those words to Ryan."

She wasn't sure if it was just her imagination but the star seemed to twinkle just a bit brighter then. She smiled.

10 | The First Wish

December 1999

"Good morning, beautiful."

Megan grinned. "Morning, Ryan," she yawned. "Why are you calling so early? You know I just got up a couple minutes ago. You're lucky I was by the phone. The ringing may have woken up my roommates."

"No, it wouldn't have. Your roommates have already gone home for their vacation as I recall. What's wrong? You're making it sound as if calling this early is really a bad thing on a Monday morning."

"What? Haven't the guys told you that it's rude to wake women up from their beauty sleep?"

He laughed. "I'll keep that in mind next time."

"Yeah right. So what's up?"

"Nothing much. I was actually wondering if you could do something for me."

"Like what?"

"Make three wishes."

"Huh? What are you talking about?"

"You heard me, Meg. Make three wishes."

"What if I don't want to?"

"At least make one."

"Fine. I wish that I didn't have to go to the hospital and intern today."

"Something I can grant perhaps?"

She laughed. "Oh all right. How about I wish I could see you right now."

"That wish I can grant. Open your door."

"What!?" Meg shrieked, leaving her bedroom and going out. "You can't be serious. I have bed hair and I'm still in my pajamas!" she said into the phone as she padded her way to the front door.

"Believe it, I'm serious," he grinned when she finally opened the door. He hung up his cell phone and swooped in to give her a huge bear hug and a kiss on the cheek. "How's my princess?"

"This princess of yours is still in shock. I wasn't expecting you until this afternoon!"

"So I felt like surprising you. Is that a crime?"

"Not in my book," she grinned, stepping out of his arms so she could shut to the door behind him. "Anyway, you know that since you came early, you have to wait a little bit for me to get ready, right?"

"Of course. Can I watch?"

"Ryan!"

"I'm kidding. I'll stay out here. What do you want for breakfast? I feel like cooking something."

She looked at him, a smile playing on her lips. "First, you surprise me by coming early, and then you say you're going to cook for me? What did I do to deserve such royal treatment?"

"Didn't anyone ever tell you to simply accept when good things come your way?"

"That's a new one on me. I'm always suspicious when good things happen if I don't deserve them."

"Well, if it helps to ease your mind, you do deserve it. After all, you put up with me."

"That's true. It takes a strong person to have to deal with the long absences in between all our very random and very short trips and infrequent phone calls."

A bit of a strained look clouded his eyes, but she brushed off his apologies before they could even surface with a wave of her hand. He smiled. "And you're just the person to understand. God, I love you, Meg," he said, kissing her on the forehead. "Now go get changed. We wouldn't want you to be late now, would we?"

She scrunched up her face. "Just the thought of having to work today when I'm technically on vacation doesn't appeal to me one bit now that you're here," she said as she turned to go to her room.

"Well, it's your fault for volunteering to come in for extra hours. I told you you should take a break."

"And when do I listen to anyone about taking a break?" she laughed, leaving Ryan in the kitchen peering into the refrigerator.

- - -

Early that afternoon, Meg sat on the couch curled up with a cookbook in her lap. She was flipping through the pages trying to find a good dessert to make for a potluck her friends were holding that night. "I don't know. These all look hard Ryan."

"You could just go out and get some ice-cream if you need to."

She turned to where he sat next to her on the

couch and gave him a look. "Ice-cream? Now? Ryan, I don't know if you've realized this but it is December."

"I've realized that, Meg. What's wrong with ice-cream? It's good to eat anytime of the year."

She shook her head and turned back down to the pages in her lap. "You sound just like my sister."

"Well it's nice to know she's normal even if her older sister isn't."

Megan lightly jabbed him in the stomach for that one. "You're not helping me here."

"Hehe, sorry about that. Here, let me take a look." Meg gave up the book to Ryan and he started flipping through the dessert section quickly. "What about a little cheesecake? Sound good?"

He pointed to the page and Meg read over his shoulder. "Actually, yeah. Make it chocolate and that'll be even better."

"Then let's get to it. I know it will have to set for awhile so we should get the ingredients now."

"Sounds good to me."

Half an hour later, the two were back in the kitchen. Ryan glanced over at Megan as she watched him get everything together onto the kitchen table. "What's the matter? You look scared."

"I hate cooking. Something always goes wrong if I try anything more complicated that heating up TV dinners or making some pasta out of a box."

"You can't be serious. You're a college student living off of that?"

She smiled sheepishly. "At least it's not ramen."

He sighed. "You're right. That is a big plus right there."

She shrugged. "Not everyone is as lucky as you to have gourmet cooking so much."

"It's not always that great. And guess who has to work out extra hard afterward to make sure I can still fit into my clothes after all the rich food?"

"Point is, you get food cooked for you on almost a daily basis. I just don't have the luxury or the time to cook for myself these days."

"Hey, don't sweat it. You're not going about this dessert alone. I'm here."

"And you promise to be the witness saying that I didn't set out to poison anyone intentionally, right?"

"Think of it as one of your chemistry experiments then. Be careful with the measurements, follow the steps exactly, and you'll get the desired end product."

"Uhh, I guess this is not the best time to tell you that chemistry was not one of my best subjects."

Ryan just laughed as the two started to open the packages and mix everything together.

- - -

That night, the two enjoyed her friends' festive dinner. The next morning, Ryan and Megan were up pretty early after having spent the night at Megan's. Ryan came out of the bathroom, still rubbing his eyes and found Megan at the kitchen table with some paperwork spread out in front of her. "What's all that?"

"Med school applications. I haven't had time to finish the small details until now that I finally have my latest grades and I really need to send them out today. They're going to be barely on time as it is. There, I made you some coffee too," she said, pointing to a mug on the counter.

Gratefully, he took it and stood behind her chair as she finished double checking every last application she had left. He chuckled slightly. "What? Afraid you won't get in anywhere? It seems like you've applied to every med school there is."

"With my grades, trying out everywhere won't hurt. I mean, I did pretty well on my MCAT's and I have a fair background of extracurricular stuff going on, but my grades..." She sighed. "Better to be safe than sorry I suppose."

"Just watch. I bet you'll get into every single one of them." He picked up the last application she'd just sealed. "Whoa... This one's going abroad. Philippines?"

Again she shrugged. "Anywhere they can take me, I'll go."

"But... It's the Philippines. That's halfway around the world."

"I've got family there."

"What about me?"

She stopped what she was doing and looked up at him, hearing something in his voice catching her attention. "Are you worried that I'll leave you?"

"Yes," he answered honestly, taking a seat next to her and putting the application back into the pile he'd taken it from.

She grabbed onto his hand and gave it a comforting squeeze. "If luck is on our side, then I won't have to go that far to get a good education. You did just bet that I'd get in everywhere I applied. Don't worry. This is only the first step in the application process. After we mail these off today, all we can do is wait. Then we can go from there, okay? Now finish your coffee and get dressed. We've got some last minute shopping to do."

She let go of his hand to finish sealing the last couple of envelopes. After draining the coffee, Ryan went to wash his mug before going back into the bathroom to change, all the while trying to ignore the little bit of doubt that he'd gotten when he'd seen the application. 'Can I handle it if she goes away that far? Then again, doesn't she go through the same thing anytime I go flying off somewhere outside the states myself? True, we know it's temporary on my part and not for years but still... Ugh, stop it, Ry. Worrying now won't help her. All you can do is hope that things will work out. And they will.' He looked at himself in the mirror. 'They have to.'

11 | The Second Wish

Ryan watched as Megan slept in his arms. For all the last minute shopping, packing, and driving around the two had done that day, he was surprisingly awake. He knew he should have been asleep right along with her; they were going to be spending the entire next day with her family and friends for Christmas Eve and again on Christmas day. Still, he couldn't help himself. He considered himself to be very lucky at the moment to have her in his life right now. She was everything he needed and wanted in a woman. She was smart and funny. She was always there to listen to him and supported him unconditionally. He knew he'd thanked her constantly for being by his side and she always smiled and said that it was all right. She wanted to be there for him because he tried to be there for her.

When he'd left her to go back home last summer, it was as if something had changed. Even though the distance was great between them, just knowing that she was missing him as much as he was missing her helped ease the pain a little. Who knew that a week or so could do so much? Who knew that months of very sporadic day trips and phone calls would help so much? Communication is key in any relationship and they had both tried their hardest to make it work. He had seen the other guys do it with their respective girlfriends and hadn't thought much about it at first, but now that he was doing the same thing himself, he could appreciate all the work they put into their commitments outside the band.

Ryan thought back to when he'd first seen the guys again after his extended vacation.

"And here is the man of the hour! Ryan, my friend. How was your little vacation?"

Ryan found himself grinning as he hugged the guys upon entering the studio. "It was good," he said, answering Josh's question.

"Only good? I would think you had a blast. I mean come on! You were in California with the sun, the beach, the lovely ladies," Connor teased.

Ryan laughed. "All right. So I had a great time. I had a lot of fun with Megan."

"I bet you did," Josh grinned, his tone suggesting something more.

"Please," he rolled his eyes. "There was none of that. I can have fun without having to go to bed with a girl."

Matt pretended to wipe an imaginary tear away from his eyes. "Aww look. It seems like Ryan has finally grown up and realized that there's more to a female than her body."

Ryan groaned. "Come on, Matt. Stop it. You guys know that I treat women with all the respect they deserve."

Connor chuckled. "We know, Ryan. We're just teasing. It's been a while since you've had a crush on someone though, so we can't help it," he said as he led them all into dance hall so they could start polishing up on their routines for the upcoming tour.

When the group had broken up for the day, Ryan

found himself jogging a little to catch up with his fellow band mate. "Hey Matt! Wait up!"

Matt turned around and paused, waiting for Ryan to catch up to him. "What's up?"

"I want you to take a look at something for me."

"Oh?" He watched as Ryan reached into a pocket and pulled out some folded sheets of paper. "What's this?" he asked.

"They're just some lyrics to a song I'm thinking about writing. It's not done but I wanted to know what you thought so far."

Matt scanned the papers and found his mouth curling up to a smile. He hummed to himself a few of the notes that were written as well, trying to get a sense of the mood Ryan wanted. He looked up. "You really like the girl, huh? You never sit down and just write music."

Ryan looked away and blushed. "She's different, Matt. To her, I'm just another normal guy."

Matt smiled. "She sounds like a keeper. Hold on to her if she means that much to you and I'll see what I can do about this," he motioned to the papers in his hand.

"Is it okay?" he asked worriedly.

"Ryan, my boy," he said, reaching around to pat his friend on the back and start leading them out of the parking lot. "It's perfect. We just have to spruce it up to make it presentable to your lady love."

Ryan smiled to himself. The two had worked here and there on the new song since then and it was slowly taking shape. He wanted it to be perfect and there was no need to rush on it. This was going to be a special song. Who knew? Maybe it could even go on the next album if it was good enough.

Ryan finally allowed himself drift off to sleep as thoughts of singing the ballad to Megan filled his head.

- - -

The day after Christmas, Megan lay on a couch in the common area as she took one of her binders in hand and started reviewing some of her notes. Without realizing it, she started humming a little melody to herself as she skimmed through pages of her handwriting. Every once in awhile, she'd stop and reach up to take the highlighter from behind her ear to highlight an important detail, or she'd take a pencil to scrawl a brief note to herself in the margin to go over something else again later in more detail.

Matt took a break from his own reading at the small kitchen area and found himself looking up at her. 'He was right,' he thought to himself. 'She's definitely not like other girls. Any other girl would have been upset at having their boyfriend gone so much. And now that they're supposed to be spending time together, she's in here studying instead of hanging with Ryan as he works out in the gym with Josh, not like I blame her for that matter, but neither of them minds. It's so amazing watching those two. When they're together, they make the cutest couple. They're inseparable and there's such a strong bond between them. She could be with her family right now and she chose to fly out here and spend some time with us, getting to know us in between our latest promotion engagements. At the same time, the two of them don't crowd each other out. They respect each other and understand that they each have their separate lives as well. They've got a good balance.

'Poor Ryan... The guys and I often joke around now that it seems like he's found the one and how he's so smitten with her. True, we were hesitant at first and with good reason. Three of us were in committed relationships before the band took off. Ryan had the hardest image to maintain here, being the lone bachelor of the group and of course we'd be wary of just anyone who'd caught his eye. I mean, at least he has a good head on his shoulders and now that we've met her... I'd have to agree, she is a special gal. We can see that now and we can truly stand behind Ryan the entire way. If nothing else, having her around these next couple of days will help me get a feel for the type of song he wants to write should be and we can finally finish it.'

Matt found himself getting up from his stool at the countertop, leaving the newspaper behind as he moved into the living room. He took a seat in a loveseat across from her and asked if she'd mind if he turned on the television. Without even glancing up, she told him that she didn't. He took the remote and started flipping through channels, finding nothing and eventually settling for a movie he'd seen just a couple weeks ago.

He resettled in his seat and found himself glancing over at Megan again. She was in the same position as before, lying on her back with her knees drawn up. One hand held the binder from the top and the other lay on her stomach, pencil in hand and highlighter tucked behind her ear. At a glance, she looked relaxed but her face held a different story. Her brow was slightly wrinkled in concentration and there was tension in her jaw. She wasn't frowning, but her mouth was set in a determined line. Her brown eyes were alert as she went over her notes again.

He didn't know how much time had passed but she somehow noticed that he wasn't paying attention to the movie and glanced up. Surprise crossed her face when she noticed him looking at her. "What?"

"Nothing."

"Then why are you looking at me, Matt?"

He tilted his head a little, never breaking his gaze from her face. "I'm just trying to figure some things out about you. Like this," he pointed at her. "You're on vacation. Why are you studying?"

"I'm pre-med. There is no such thing as vacation." She caught the look he gave her and grinned. "Don't look so shocked. This isn't hard core studying. I'm just reviewing some things that I should have known for finals."

"Oh. But those classes are over though, right?"

"Uh huh, but it doesn't hurt to keep my mind refreshed on these things."

"Okay."

"So what else?"

"Huh?"

"You said you were trying to figure stuff out about me. You've got the studying down. What else would you like to know?"

"I don't know if there's really anything else you

can tell me."

"Oh?"

"Yeah. I mean I'm just wondering what it is about you that Ryan's so crazy about. No offense, you seem like a nice enough person."

"It's just that you don't know me well enough yet huh? Don't worry. I understand. I ask the same things when my friends start seeing someone seriously."

"So you aren't upset?"

"Of course not. Just tell me one thing."

"Shoot."

"If you ever find out why exactly he likes me, let me know. I don't know why either," she grinned before turning back to her binder.

- - -

"Yesterday was good," Ryan was saying to Josh from where he lay on his back, doing some bench pressing.

"Yeah? But come on! Weren't you freaked out about meeting her parents and all?" Josh asked in reply as he stood above his friend, spotting him.

"Name a guy who hasn't been scared out of their mind when meeting their girlfriend's family for the first time. Of course it was nerve racking, but I think it turned out well enough. I think Megan had a plan introducing me first to her sister and just spending time with them so I could get used to the idea of the family first. Those two are really close and they made me feel comfortable. Meeting their parents was still hard but for some reason, it was easier I guess."

"Well that's good. I give her props for spoon feeding you to her family."

Ryan laughed. "Well it's nice to know that you're thinking well of her."

"She's all right. I mean give me credit. I've only been hesitant about this whole relationship between you two because I only ever saw her for an hour maybe two here and there when she could fly out to watch one of our shows or something until today."

"What about you, Connor? What do you think?" he asked the youngest member of the group as soon as he spotted him walking towards them with a towel thrown over his shoulder and a bottle of water in hand.

"About Megan? I agree with Josh. She seems okay so far, but then again, we haven't had as much time with her as you just yet you know," he grinned.

"I know, but I wanted to hear what kind of impression she's been given you guys already," Ryan smiled back.

"Impression? Why are you asking us?" Connor questioned. "Are you having doubts or something?"

"No. I just want to know if I had the support of two of my closest friends."

"Sorry if we nagged you these past few months, Ryan," Josh answered. "We just wanted to make sure you weren't setting yourself up to get hurt. Long-distance relationships are hard."

"I know that. I'm reminded of that fact every time I hear you talk about your little girl and Connor and Matt complain about being away from their respective loves. And I know it's even harder this time of the year when none of them wanted to do the whole fly in and out of random cities for this holiday promo we're in the middle of."

"But now at least you won't be alone with just us anymore," Connor chuckled. "You can finally join the rest of us in our moaning and griping."

Ryan smiled back.

- - -

"You know, I like having you in my arms like this," Ryan said as the two sat on his couch, curled up together in front of the fireplace the day after New Year's.

"Mm hmm," she agreed, cuddling up closer to him as he kissed her softly on the neck.

"You're liking this, huh?"

"Why wouldn't I be? For once, I've got you all to myself. No family to show off to and meet, either yours or mine. No more TV appearances to be made. And as much as I like the guys, they're not here either. It's just you and me and a white winter outside. It's been awhile since we just relaxed."

"With the holiday season here, what would you expect?"

"Nothing else, I suppose."

"So what? Are you happy?"

"Of course I am. I just wish I didn't have to go back home tomorrow. This you and me time with just us is so little."

"Well you do have two wishes left. Say the word and we could book you a later flight."

"Ryan, you do realize how expensive flying is at

this time of year, right?"

"And you know money's not an issue here."

"But you spoil me enough already. I don't need to be pampered so much."

"You just don't want to spend more time with me, huh?"

She playfully jabbed him in the stomach. "You're so funny sometimes. This just isn't one of them."

"Ouch. That hurt."

"Poor baby. I've forgotten how sensitive you can be."

"Seriously though. Just say the word and we can call the airline now."

"As tempting as that sounds, I really have to decline the offer."

"You don't like me after all, huh?"

"Goof. You know classes start up on Monday."

"I know, I know. You remind me of that fact all too often for me to forget anyway."

"And that's only because you supposedly keep forgetting."

"When it comes to you? Yeah right. I never forget when it comes to you."

"Liar."

"Uh uh, I don't lie to you, remember?"

"Fine. Flirt then."

"Definitely, but only with you."

"You're just sucking up, trying to get some brownie points, aren't you?"

"I know from the guys that I'll need them at one time or another."

She laughed. "Wow, a guy who's been pre-trained. It almost takes the fun out of it."

"Hey!"

"I did say almost," she pointed out.

"So what's your point? I do believe you just lost of some of your brownie points with me."

"Oh whatever. As if 'I' would be the one to cause the downfall in this relationship. It's always the guy's fault."

"Well this guy will not be the one to break this relationship apart. You're lucky I love you too much to let you go."

"I know I'm lucky. That's why I don't think I'll be needing my last two wishes."

"Aww, now who's not being fun?"

"Fine, fine. One wish. I'll save my last wish for something good."

"Fair enough. It's been a couple of weeks since I granted your first wish."

"Mm hmm."

"Any ideas on what you want for your next wish then?"

"Actually, yeah," she said after a moment's thought.

"So tell me. What does your heart desire right now?"

She blushed lightly. "It's kinda silly."

"Just tell me and if I can do it, I'll do it, save for going out in the cold right now in case I get a cold."

"Aww, you wouldn't get sick for me?"

"Unless you'd be willing to take care of me until I get better, then I'd really appreciate staying healthy for you."

She laughed. "Fine, fine."

"So what do you want?"

"Promise me you won't laugh?"

"Is it that bad?"

"Please, Ryan."

"All right. I promise I won't laugh."

"Okay. Would you mind singing for me then?"

He smiled gently. "That's it?"

"Yes please."

"Is that an official wish?"

"Uh huh. I wish for you to sing me a song right now."

"Well I guess since you asked so nicely, I could do that."

"Thank you," she smiled sweetly.

"Anything for you, Megan, my dear. Any requests?"

"Anything but your latest single actually. I think I've heard that a bit too much lately around you guys."

He chuckled. "I told you that you didn't have to come see us perform."

"Naw. I wanted to come and show my support."

"Then don't complain about hearing us perform the same thing over and over again."

"And saying the same thing, interview after interview," she laughed. "I'm not complaining. I just want to hear something different."

"Aah, something different to appease her highness." Another weak jab to his midsection warned him to lighten up with the teasing. "All right, all right," he laughed. "What to sing, what to sing…" he said to himself, unconsciously drawing Megan closer to him. He closed his eyes and rested his head on her shoulder, humming a little to himself as he tried to find the perfect song. He smiled to himself when the perfect song came into mind.

> *Memorable, that's what you are.*
> *Always in my thoughts, though here or not.*
> *The memory of your warm love embraces me,*
> *Keeps me inspired to be more me.*
> *I cannot recall when someone has been more*
> *Memorable to me.*
> *Forever, you shall be*
> *Imprinted in my mind for eternity.*
> *Darling, mine, it's almost unbelievable*
> *That you feel the way I do,*
> *The way I feel about you.*

Ryan lifted her hand to his lips and planted a soft kiss onto her skin. Megan blushed a little as she smiled. "Thanks, Ryan. Usually, I don't like that song but from you, I like it."

"Anything for my princess," he replied, smiling down at her before giving her a sweet kiss.

12 | The Proclamation

As Megan and Ben walked out hand in hand after the concert, a lone figure stepped out into the light. "Megan."

She turned and immediately smiled, running the few feet that separated them. "You're here! You came!"

Ryan held her body close to his, breathing in the scent that he only knew to be hers. "Of course I came. I couldn't miss you performing for the world."

She drew back, giving him a quick peck on the cheek and started leading him to the other man who'd accompanied her out. "Ryan, you remember Ben, right? He plays viola and also works with me at the hospital."

As the two gave each other brief hellos, a fellow chorus member called out. "Hey! You coming to the post-concert get-together, Meg?"

A quick glance at Ryan, and she made her mind. As comfortable as he was with her immediate friends and family, he still didn't want to take the chance and create a scene when he was out on his own. "Not this time. I have other plans." She turned to the guys. "Hey, why don't you go on, Ben? It'll be fun."

"I've said it once and I'll say it again," Ben began

as she began bouncing on her toes. "You're too energetic after a concert is over."

"It's the natural high, what can I say? So are you going? I know that some of the other orchestra members are going."

"I know, and I'd love to go but I have an early shift tomorrow at the hospital and you know how Dr. Keen feels if we're late."

"That's true. Oh well. I guess I'll just see you later then, Ben."

"Right. Bye Megan, Ryan," he said as the couple walked on towards her car without him.

They made their way back to her home so she could pack her backpack with a few things before heading to the hotel he'd booked so as not to bother her roommates with their being up.

"You know, you're lucky I don't have to get up early tomorrow," Megan called from the bathroom where she was washing up from that night.

"Good. Does that mean we can wake up at say nine or ten then?"

"Of course not. Well, you can I suppose, and I can just work on some things while you sleep."

"Aah, you're killing me, Meg. You almost make me feel guilty with all the work you do. Do you ever take a break?"

"Do you?" she asked back with a grin.

He laughed from where he sat inside the bedroom part of the suite and she smiled in the bathroom where she was toweling dry her face. When she came out, she found him looking through her a photo album she'd brought along to share with him. "Where'd you take these pictures?" he asked her.

Megan glanced over to where Ryan was sitting. "Oh that? That was last month at a banquet Ben and I went to. Remember the one where all the graduates of the health club on campus get recognized? I thought I told you about it."

"You did," he nodded. "You and Ben went together?"

"Yeah. Just as friends though, don't worry," she smiled, seeing a frown start to form on his face before she said that.

"Good," he smiled back. "Getting ready for bed?" he asked, noticing how she was already dressed in her pajamas.

"Yup," she nodded. "I think the rush is finally wearing off. What about you? I'm surprised jet lag hasn't hit you this time."

"I think your energy rubbed off on me but yeah, I'm getting tired too now that you mention it," he replied, shutting the album and putting it aside to climb into bed with her. "Did I tell you that you did a wonderful job tonight?"

"Oh please, Ryan. I bet you couldn't even hear me in the chorus, especially with our huge soprano section."

"I didn't hear you sticking out and singing terribly off so that must mean you sang well."

She poked him in the stomach with her elbow. "Big meanie."

She felt him chuckle. "Good night, Meg."

"Good night, Ryan."

- - -

The next morning found Megan up by eight. Ryan woke up some time later and almost panicked when he noticed how she was no longer in his arms. Quickly, he turned over and relaxed when he saw Megan at the desk working already. He watched her for a few minutes as she flipped through a few sheets of paper and made notes for herself. She looked so intense, he had to get up and see what she was doing. One glance though and he felt his heart drop a little. "More applications?"

Megan looked up, startled. "Ryan! Good morning!"

He took the other seat and the small stack of papers with him, making Meg take a break. Slowly, he himself went through the pile, page by page. It wasn't an application at all. It was an acceptance letter, and she was replying to agree to go to that school.

"You're really going to do it? Go abroad to the Philippines?" He looked up to her, an indescribable look on his face.

"Yeah," she smiled. "I already talked to my family and they and I agree that this'd be the best thing for me."

"But what about any of the other schools? Didn't you get accepted into any of those?"

"Uh huh. A few actually, and a few of them even offered me some scholarships."

"So then why go so far?"

"Even with the scholarships, it's a lot of money. We can't afford it with my sister starting college in the fall. We're lucky she's getting a bunch of scholarships for that but it still wouldn't be enough.

Financially, this is the best way, and I'd still be getting a quality education."

"You'd be gone for four years?"

She shrugged. "It depends. I've always been interested in specializing, although I'm not sure in what and going that route would add at least a couple more years minimum. But that's still too far down the road for me to think about," she said, taking back her papers so she could keep filling them out.

"I don't want you to go."

"I know, Ryan, but it's going to be okay," she said as she checked the box, agreeing to go to that school.

"No really. I don't want you to go, Meg."

"Ryan," she said, looking up at him briefly and wondering what was wrong. "I'm going. It's not up to debate."

"But you never told me this."

"You were there when I filled out the application!"

"And you said that this'd be a last resort and we'd talk about it."

"We are talking about it. Ryan, I thought you'd be happy for me. I got accepted and I'm going to med school!"

"I am happy for you, Meg, but I just don't like the idea of you having to cross an entire ocean to get there."

"I told you already. I have family there who will watch out for me so I won't be completely lost. I know I have to brush up on the language but that won't be too hard either. Also, I happen to like the place. They have clothes there that I can buy and actually wear without tailoring them some way," she tried to joke.

It didn't work. "Megan, it's hard enough traveling to California to see you, but the Philippines is an almost twenty hour flight from where I am!"

Megan tried to bite back her tongue and paused a few moments before choosing what to say next. "I'm not asking you to fly over there. I never asked you to fly over here either. I know you have a busy schedule and so do I. We both knew going into this that long distance relationships are hard but we do it anyway. We both fly out to see each other because we want this to work, but it's not like we see each other all too often anyway so how different will this be?"

"It will be very different, Meg. Can you imagine the scene when I step off the plane in Manila and find myself to be the only Caucasian guy there? You know we're big in Asia too and that's just asking for trouble."

She couldn't hide her wince this time. "So don't go then," she said as she started packing up her paperwork into her backpack.

"Come on, Meg. Now you're just being silly." A worried look crossed his face as he watched her, her face stormy with emotions he rarely saw in her.

"Am I, Ryan? I hadn't noticed," she said as she stood up.

"I just don't want you to go because I think it'll be too hard for both of us."

"I know I'm perfectly capable of this. I'm more

than willing to make the sacrifices. It's what I do. What you're saying is that this will be hard for you, you mean."

"What? Of course not."

"You know the world doesn't revolve around you."

"I know it doesn't. Meg, where are you −" he watched as she crossed the room to put on her shoes. "No, you're not going anywhere until we finish −" he reached out to grab a hold of her hand.

"Finish what, Ryan? I don't ask you to make any sacrifices for me, but you want me to just sit here and listen to you saying I can't go because you don't want me to? No. I have better things to do than that," she said as she pulled out of his grasp.

"Meg, listen to me. That's not what I meant."

"Then what did you mean? Because the way I understand things, it doesn't sound like this relationship is worth the trouble for you. You know, you were the best thing that came into my life recently." Ryan winced at her use of the past tense. "But if all the sacrifice wasn't worth it, then let me know right now."

"I wasn't trying to say that."

"I don't want to hear what you were trying to say. I want to know if you think this relationship is worth it or not."

"Meg…"

She shook her head angrily, not trusting her voice in the moment. She brushed him off when he tried again to get a grip on her as she passed by, her backpack slung over her shoulder.

"Wait! Where are you going?"

"I'm off to study," she answered, not glancing back at him. "It's time I rearranged my priorities seeing as you don't hold me high on your list."

"No, that's not what I said," he called after her but she was already out the door. Cursing to himself, he rushed to pull on some sweats over his boxers and stuff his feet into his shoes before rushing out after her. Those few seconds were enough to let her reach her car, throw in her stuff, and turn on the ignition. Without a backwards glance, she pulled out of the parking lot even as he tried to run after her. "Megan..." he puffed out, stopping after only a few feet. He watched as her car disappeared into traffic.

13 | Rotten Apples

She had never seen her this angry before. It frightened her how dark Meg's eyes were and how she still shook with her pent up rage. She could only imagine how her daughter had managed to drive all the way to her childhood home without getting into an accident. "Meg! What are you doing home?"

"I needed to get away."

"What happened? Did something happen at school? At the hospital? Are you roommates okay? Friends?"

"Ryan."

Her mom took a step back and watched Meg pace in the living room. She was surprised. What could Ryan have done to get her this upset? When she'd met him, she saw how attentive he was to her and how he had a genuine interest in her daughter. The two got along great and it seemed like she had met her match. "What happened, honey?"

"He said that this relationship wasn't worth the trouble."

"What? I can't believe he'd say something like that."

"He didn't say it in those words no, but he might as well have. He was going off on how much trouble it'll be seeing each other while I'm at med school. You should have been there, but I'm sure you can imagine how I felt just an hour ago. The things I put up for the guy. The distance, the media and other fan girls, our careers and futures in mind…"

"Meg, calm down! I'm sure you're just emotionally charged right now. How did Ryan even come to say such things? Isn't he back home?"

"No. He came here yesterday to see us perform."

"Well that was sweet of him."

Meg glared at her mom. "That's beside the point."

"Is it?" she asked skeptically. "Meg, did you actually try to rationalize this yet or did you just let your anger overrule your mind?"

"Probably," she answered grudgingly. "But that doesn't hide the fact that he didn't say yes either."

"Yes to what, dear?"

"I asked him if he thought that this was worth all the sacrifice and he didn't answer. Mom, it was a simple yes or no answer and he didn't say anything!" she said, finally turning to her mom and coming to a stop from her pacing. Megan's mom took the cue and opened up her arms for her daughter as she finally just gave up and started crying. "What am I going to do? I just left him like that."

"Shh… There, there," she said as she patted her daughter. "Just cry first. You need to get this out. You've been holding this in for awhile now."

"I thought he'd be supportive. I thought he'd understand how important this is for me."

"Hush. I'm sure he knows, more so now than before perhaps, but what can you expect? This must have been a big shock for him. Haven't you guys talked about this before now?"

"Not really, there were always other things to talk about, it kind of slipped my mind with classes and getting ready for the last of my finals and his crazy schedule. But he was being so selfish. He didn't want me to go just because he didn't want me to go."

"Meg, anybody, especially a boyfriend, would say that when first hearing the news."

She was quiet for a while as she let her mother's words sink in. "I was irrational then, huh?"

"The two of you probably said and did things that you both will regret for awhile."

"I think I did more of the regrettable stuff than he. At least he was being honest."

"And I'm sure you were too. First reactions usually are."

"But he wasn't the one to walk out on the situation," Meg pointed out. She sighed and rested her head in her hands. "I have to go back. If there's some way to fix this, I have to now. Waiting never did help anybody."

"Are you sure you have to go now? You're still pretty emotional right now. I don't want you driving off like this."

"I'll be fine, mom."

After trying to reason with her daughter some more and getting nowhere, Megan's mom gave in. "All right. Just be careful. Let me know when you get there."

"I will. Thanks for talking with me," she said as she was walking out the door.

"I'm your mother. I'll always be here for you to talk to." The two hugged and parted their ways, mother watching as daughter struggled to piece together a shattered world.

- - -

The first thing Meg did when she got back to town was go to the hotel to see if Ryan was still there. When no one answered the door, she went back out to the lobby to ask the receptionist. "Excuse me? I was wondering if the person in room 215 is still here."

"Hold on, let me check," he answered as he turned to the computer. After a few clicks, he shook his head. "I'm sorry ma'am. He checked out before noon."

"Oh." Megan's heart fell even more. "Do you remember how he left?"

"Yes, actually. I called for a cab for him to take him to the airport."

"I see." All hope of reconciling in face pretty much left her right then. "Umm, thanks anyway."

"I'm sorry I wasn't more help ma'am. Have a good day."

"Thanks. You too."

Megan walked back out into the sunlight and stopped for a moment. 'The airport? Meg my dear, you've just screwed yourself over big time.' She looked skyward. 'Ryan, wherever you are, I'm sorry. I really am. I will fix this…'

- - -

"Hey, Ryan. How was the concert?"

Ryan gave a small smile as he entered the studio to meet with the guys later that evening. "The concert was good. They did an awesome job," he answered Josh.

"And Megan? Did you get a chance to sing her the song yet?" Matt asked.

He took a seat at one microphone and shook his head. "Not yet."

"How come? It's ready. I would have thought –"

"Hey guys?" Their producer called for their attention from the other room. "Enough chit-chat. Time to record. Let's start with the new one."

Ryan, relieved of having to go through the interrogation for the moment, nodded along with the rest of the guys as they waited for their cue to start singing. As Matt finished wrapping up the first verse, Ryan had to close his eyes to prepare. The mental image of Meg smiling at him from the night before just wouldn't come up though. All he could remember was the anger she had thrown at him that morning. He sighed.

Connor took notice of the reserved bass and nudged his friend. "You okay?" he mouthed so as not to disturb Matt, who was singing his part again.

Ryan looked up and saw Connor's concerned look directed toward him. He had to nod and give a small smile. He didn't want to worry them, but he knew that he hadn't convinced the young one at all. He shrugged and mouthed 'later' before turning to the microphone to start harmonizing with the rest of them as the cue came for them to start singing.

As soon as the recording session was done for that day, Ryan tried his best to leave the guys without their noticing. They wouldn't have it. Connor, Josh, and Matt had all noticed that something was up and tried to get the bass to talk to them. "Guys really. I just want to go home. It's been a long day, especially with the flight. Besides, I have to go unpack."

"Unpack what? You were gone for less than a day!" Josh pointed out.

"Guys, please. I just want to be on my own right now."

"No. What did she do?" Matt demanded, hating to see his friend in so much distress and immediately wanting to help if he could.

"What makes you think she had anything to do with this?" The guys gave him a pointed stare. "Okay, so we had a little bit of an argument this morning. Nothing to worry about," he said even as the image of Megan walking out his hotel door popped up in his mind and he felt his heart tear apart some more. He tried his best to ignore the worried looks his friends were giving. "Guys, really. I just need to think this through on my own for at least a night. I'll talk to you guys in the morning, I swear. For now, just leave me alone." Hurt looks crossed his friends' faces but he'd already brushed his way past them. He felt terrible. It was rare for him to lose his temper like that, but to lash out to three of his best friends? He sighed and shook his head as he started his car. "Go figure I'd lose it over a girl," he said to himself.

Even before he had stepped inside his home though, Ryan knew what would be waiting for him when he got back. He finally powered on his phone for the first time since getting on the airplane and a notification let him know he was right. Taking a look at voicemail box, he knew instantly that Megan had called to leave a message. He stared at the icon for a moment, hesitant. He didn't know if he could take another of her angry fits. She'd frightened him earlier. He knew she was passionate about what she wanted to do. What right did he have to take that away from her? He could understand why she was so upset, but to have all that anger and fury directed to him? He never wanted to go through that again if he could help it.

At the same time, if she had called to apologize, he didn't know if he could forgive her for hurting him like that so soon. She got to be honest with her emotions. He hadn't been given much of a chance to speak what was going on in his own mind, granted he'd just gotten up and was still half asleep and in denial when they'd been arguing.

He braced himself as he pressed the play button.

"Hey Ryan," the recording started. "It's Meg. I really don't want to do this over the phone, but I just got home from the hotel and they said that you'd gone to the airport already. I can only assume that that means you went home. Look, I'm sorry. Words cannot even begin to describe how I terrible I feel right now. I was irrational and angry this morning. It was wrong of me to have assumed that you believed the relationship to not be worth it and then accuse you of it before you could even say a word in your defense. I am so, so sorry. I don't know what got into me earlier. It's just... I don't know. Maybe we're not cut out for this long distance thing. It's one thing when we're at least in the same country the majority of the time, you're right. And I thought we were doing fine enough as it was, but I guess not, or at least, I don't know anymore. I really don't. I don't know what else to say, what to do... I don't know. Maybe we need a break. You've got your stuff going for you and I know you guys are going to be in the studio for a while getting the next album recorded and all. Me, there's a couple of weeks left before school and then finals and then graduation... But you knew that already. Ryan..." She paused and he could almost feel the frustration she had with herself as she sighed. "I don't know. I'm sorry, Ryan. I really am."

Ryan looked down at the phone as the message cut off, letting him know that that was it. There were no other missed calls, no other new voicemails to listen to. He slowly exhaled the breath that he'd been holding and let his shoulders slump forward. Without another glance to the phone, he dropped it on the stand in the hallway and trudged off in the direction of his room.

14 | Mirror, Mirror

June 2000

"Megan."

A stern voice crashed through her dulled senses and she straightened up to find herself facing her instructor. "Dr. Keen! Is there something I can do for you?"

She hurried to stand up but found the woman indicating she stay seated, surprising Megan further by taking a seat in a chair nearby. "I'm concerned about you."

"Me? Did I do something wrong? I don't know what I did but it must be important. I promise you, I'll fix it, whatever it is, or make it up the best way I can-"

"Megan, calm down. You're not in trouble." It took Megan a slow second to register that bit of information and she tried to relax as she waited to hear what the doctor had come to tell her. "That's better. As I was about to say, and I don't know how else to put it, I think you need a break."

"But Doctor-"

"I won't hear otherwise, Megan. You've been in this hospital more often than not lately and while I appreciate the dedication, it's not healthy for a young woman like you."

"Dr. Keen, I come here because I want to be here.

I have a responsibility to you and everyone else in the department and I can't just take off. There's so much to be done."

"And the other interns can take care of it for you while you're away. They need to shape up if they want any recommendations from me anyway."

"Please, Dr. Keen. I don't want to go."

Her superior looked at her and saw that Megan really didn't want to go out there, and for a moment, the elder woman's face softened. "You only have a week left here, Megan. It's all right. You've shown your dedication and your passion for your work here and I'd still be more willing to write up whatever letters of recommendation you need now or in the future. But Megan, you're hiding from something that's out there, and I want you to go and solve whatever it is that's bothering you. You know your attitude is reflected in your work here, and while I know you've been trying to hide it from everyone, you're not doing a good enough of a job. A lot of people are worried about you and that includes me. Whatever it is, we're behind you all the way, but the only way you can solve this is to work on it and not hide behind your work here. Believe me, you'll be much happier in the long run."

"But Doctor-"

"Not another word, Megan. I don't want to see you here until next week." She stood up, indicating that she was done with her for the time being. She hesitated though, seeing the lost look in Megan's eyes. Dr. Keen laid a comforting hand on top of Meg's clenched ones. "Go. I promise it'll all be okay."

Megan looked into the doctor's eyes and nodded after a second. Numb, Megan stood up and went to get her things to leave.

- - -

"What did Dr. Keen say to you?" Ben asked as he caught up with Megan as she was walking out of the break room and out the clinic doors.

"Other than the fact that I've been banned from the hospital until I am deemed emotionally stable enough to come back?" she tried to joke, but her laugh was only half-hearted and the sadness she felt closed in on her even tighter.

"Megan," he said, drawing her shaking body close to his, letting her cry. When she was in more control of herself, he gently asked where her keys were. When she opened a palm, he took the keys out. "Come on. Let's get you home."

Only then did Megan begin to try and snap out of things. "Ben! What about your work? I can drive myself home. You don't have to-"

"Don't argue with me, Meg. I'd feel better knowing you weren't driving when you're feeling like this. Besides, Dr. Keen told me to."

"Everyone thinks I'm really going crazy, huh?" she asked, a hurt look on her face.

"Megan," he took her by the shoulders and forced her to look at him. "You're not crazy. You're just hurting. And you've got a lot of people worried about you, the staff, the patients… We care about you, Meg. Don't forget that."

Staring into his eyes, Meg could tell he was

being sincere and was trying desperately to help her in any way he could. As a classmate, he'd come to know her as a hard worker, dedicated to her studies and her music. Working with her, he'd come to know her passion for helping others. All the time in between, he'd come to know her as friend, and even girlfriend for just a little while in the past, finding the quirks that made Meg who she was. He'd loved her then, and loved her now. Slowly, she nodded and let him hug her again before being guided to the passenger door.

The ride home was silent.

- - -

"Lori! What are you doing here?" Meg asked when she opened the door and found her best friend standing outside.

"I got a call from Ben and he told me it was important that I come," she answered, stepping inside.

"But your work at the internship!"

She shrugged. "You're more important that that." Lori spied a suitcase in the hallway. "Packing already?"

"Not yet. I actually just got back an hour ago."

"From…"

"The mountains."

"No wonder no one could get a hold of you. Megan, you had us all worried sick!"

"I know, but I had to get away. Staying here…" She gave a vague gesture towards the rest of the house. "Even if it is empty now that my roommates have packed up and left, I just didn't think this place would be the best place for me to think. There are just too many memories here, in this town…"

"But the mountains? You do not just isolate yourself completely like that unless it's something really big."

"I needed the time and quiet to think, and I knew I could get that there."

"Meg, what happened?"

She clenched her jaw for a moment, unsure of how to answer. "Ryan and I…" She shrugged. "We got into a fight."

"So? Little disagreements happen all the time. And I know you, Meg. You don't let them trip you up like that. You work hard to make sure everything gets better so what's up?"

"This wasn't just a little disagreement, Lori. This was me accusing him of having no faith in our relationship. This was me not giving him a chance to say otherwise because I was too self-centered to even listen to myself close enough to hear what I was saying. This was me walking out on him. A few hours later, it was me finding out he'd left for home and then me calling to apologize… But the damage was done. Lori, that was last week and I haven't heard from him since. I messed this up and lost him because I pushed him away. Now do you see why I needed to get away?"

Fresh tears spilled from Meg's eyes as Lori gave her best friend a hug. "I don't know what else to do now, Lori. I've thought about flying over there before I leave in a couple weeks but seeing as I haven't heard from him either way to know if he's angry or just as upset as I am..."

"You know if you don't talk to him before you leave though, you'll always be wondering what if."

"I don't know, Lori. I just don't know. What else is there for me to say? I've apologized but the silence from his end is absolutely killing me. Where to go from there..." She shrugged. "Maybe this is a good way to end it after all. He was right. The distance between here and his home was far enough. Crossing an entire ocean on top of that would put more stress and strain in this relationship than it's worth."

"Come on, Meg. Do you honestly believe that?"

"I've got to," she said, giving a watery smile. "It's the only way to keep me from crying myself to sleep every night."

- - -

A few weeks later, Meg stood in front of her bathroom mirror one last time and a tired woman stared back. For those who did not know her, they assumed that she was just tired from all the packing she had had to do. Not only did she have to pack up everything from her house for the people moving in, but she had to go home and pack up her stuff there for her big move overseas. What she couldn't take or didn't need, she put away in storage.

But her exhaustion went deeper than that. The knowledge that she had hurt Ryan weighed on her more, and the only thing keeping going was her friends' and family's faith in her. Their support was unconditional, and she knew she'd be eternally grateful for it.

With one last look at herself, Meg turned and left the bathroom. She grabbed one last suitcase and walked outside to pack it into her full car. One quick run through of the house showed her that the place was truly empty and so, she locked the front door one last time. She placed the key in an envelope addressed to the new owners and dropped it off with them where they were in the process of getting ready to move as well. With one last matter to get to, Meg stopped by the post office.

She looked at the envelope in her hands, still undecided on either to send it or not. It had taken so much energy to write the letter inside, to make sure that it said what she really needed it to say… She slowly traced Ryan's name on the envelope with her finger and then forced herself to quickly drop the letter into the mailbox before she could stall anymore. Without looking back, she left the place she'd called home for four years and drove herself to the airport where she'd be taking the next step towards her future, which, once upon a time looked very bright. Now, she just wasn't so sure…

15 | Love Songs

November 2002

"*You are my heart's song*," the guys sang as they stood in the sand. "*Your love is the magic potion that makes this fairy tale come true.*"

Ryan tried to focus on his job. He smiled toward the camera when he noticed it pointing his way. He walked through his scenes with the appropriate saddened look on his face. But when he watched as Matt and Connor and Josh go through their scenes...

He didn't miss the irony of the whole ordeal. The song he and Matt had written together and had been the one Ryan was supposed to have sung to Meg that morning... It was only appropriate that the others got to share the screen with the loves of their lives and have those moments captured on film. For him... He had resumed his status as official bachelor of the group once more, and his scene offered him a sense of peace and closing, for love past and still going on in a more metaphorical sense.

If he was honest with himself, he knew he was bothered that it wasn't Megan there with him on set, comforting him in the video shoot as the director wanted. Frankly, Ryan would have rather gone through the scene alone to deal with his scene of saying goodbye to his grandmother, but the director wanted him to have a pretty girl. And so they'd gotten him a pretty girl. 'Even if this is more staged than reality, I wonder what Meg will think when she sees this video,' he thought to himself. And then he sighed. 'Knowing Meg, she probably doesn't have the time to even think about me or watch the video.' Ryan forced himself to snap out of it. The director was calling everyone in to discuss something else and he made his way over.

Matt caught his glance. It wasn't lost on the guys how hard singing this piece was for the bass. Matt was especially concerned. It had been difficult enough getting him to agree to include the track on the new CD because it was so personal, but to also release it as a single as well? He didn't know how Ryan was doing it, holding it all together. 'Then again, it's been a couple years now since he and Megan last talked. Time may be a good healer, but those two never really closed anything either. It's just there.' Unconsciously, he squeezed his fiancé Jessica's hand a little bit, ever thankful she was there with her love and support, and was rewarded with a brilliant smile. 'I just hope Ryan finds this kind of happiness soon. A friend can only watch someone else go through only so much pain…'

- - -

February 2003

"With all the work you've done, Meg, I don't see why you wouldn't be able to go yourself. This all happened because of you, you know."

"I know, but I wanted to make sure and ask anyway. It's all so unbelievable."

"Well, it was all about the timing. You did the research and all the extra work. The only things the school really needed were a general interest, which of course wasn't hard to find, and doctors who've been through our program and have settled over in the states."

"And the fact that most of them were more than willing to participate was a great incentive."

"Exactly. It's a help to them to have students willing to learn and a great opportunity for you students to get more hands on experience. So the only thing you have to worry about is the fact that you'll technically be a foreign student over there even though you are a citizen of the states. That shouldn't be too much of a big deal though. Just the normal mountain of paperwork to deal with next," he laughed.

She smiled. "I still can't believe it."

"Well believe it, Megan. You did it. Congratulations."

"Thanks. I couldn't have done it without you," she said to one of her professors.

"It was my pleasure. Now you better get going. I thought you had an exam coming up in a few weeks."

"That I do. I'll see you in class tomorrow then. Thanks again!" She waved good-bye as she left his office and began to make her way back to her dorm room. Once there, she found herself greeted by a handful of anxious faces. "Hey guys."

"So?" One guy asked.

"So what, Edwin?" she asked back, smiling.

"Is there a program or not?"

"Do you really have to ask?" she answered, laughing.

"Oh my god! That means they said yes!"

Her friends all began to cheer and laugh right along with Megan as they rushed forward to swallow her in a big group hug. Edwin himself came close for a hug and ended up kissing her on the cheek, surprising her when he wouldn't let her go. "Edwin! I thought we agreed to none of that."

"I know," he grinned sheepishly. "But you've got to know how proud I am of you right now. You did it! You convinced the board to let us expand our international program." He gave her another squeeze before letting her go.

"I didn't do it alone. All of you helped me out."

"Always the modest one. Come on. Let's go out for dinner tonight. We need to celebrate." Her friends quickly agreed and the fun continued over to a nearby restaurant.

After relaxing with her friends, Megan found herself back in her room alone at last later that night. As she settled herself into her chair, she reached over to her radio and turned it on low for some background music. Books and papers lined her desk against the wall and she took one book out to start studying. After gathering a few sheets of paper together, she flipped the text open to one page and began skimming the lines for important details. An unfamiliar song caught her attention a few minutes later though and she looked up toward her radio.

You say I don't need you, but I'm crying here in bed.
You say I don't need you, but your name echoes ever in
my head.
I know you're for me because my heart beats solely for
your call.
I know you're for me 'cause you're the one giving me
the strength to bear it all.

I cannot imagine what the future holds.
But knowing that you are over there, I pray that we'll
come together soon.
In the meantime, I'm hoping to be the one you share
this journey with,
Wishing you'll be the one I grow with,
Praying you'll be the one I build my dreams with.
I imagine loving you all my life.

I refuse to run away. I can't bear it. I can't
comprehend
The thought that we are not made for each other when
my heart tells me that we are.
Is there hope for me to stay with you beyond my
dreams?

For I need you, with a desire so strong that it keeps me
from breathing.
I hold you in my heart and call for the strength to
continue on again today.
I love you, no matter how long the fight.
And although I can't see you right now, please know
my heart is yours.

As the chorus repeated, Megan couldn't help but start tearing up. An image of the face she had tried so hard to forget when she moved abroad formed in her mind... But the details were sketchy. Any trace of her evening's happiness vanished when she realized just how good of a job she had done in blocking so many memories of Ryan from her mind. But she remembered the look of hurt and shock in his eyes when she left him that morning. That was something she just couldn't forget.

Megan put her pen down and sat back in her chair. She glanced at her calendar and noticed that it was the twenty-fifth. 'Why does that date sound so familiar,' she wondered. A memory of her surprising Ryan swirled in her head.

"Ryan!"

"Megan? What are you doing here?" he asked as he threw open the door and stepped outside to swing her around and kiss her soundly.

"If I had known I'd be greeted like that every time I surprised you, I would have done it more often," she laughed.

"Seriously though. Shouldn't you be studying at home?"

"I studied on the plane ride over and I'll study on the way back. No biggie."

"But Meg," he started to whine playfully.

"Oh hush, Ryan," she smiled, effectively silencing him by placing a finger to his lips. "Complain anymore and I won't give you your birthday present."

"Having you in my arms like this is present enough."

She laughed as the two finally stepped inside.

Meg's tears were flowing freely now, slipping down her face in a slow, steady stream. 'It's been so long since I've cried like this. Why now?', she wondered. 'God, do I still miss him this much? It's been over two years! Stop fooling yourself. You know you still miss him like crazy. Why else would you feel so guilty about Edwin? Come on, Meg! There's a boy here who is head over heels in love with you! And while that's true, my heart doesn't belong to him. I still love Ryan,' she argued with herself.

And then she stopped. 'Did I just admit that to myself?' She groaned. 'This is the last thing you need in your life, Meg. As if there wasn't enough going on in your life right now. There's school, there's this program you helped put together...'

She sighed. 'Do I tell Ryan?' The phone lay nearby, tempting her. She quickly did the math in her head. 'No, still a bit too early in the morning yet. Besides, how odd would it be for you to just call up? I can see it now.' "Hey Ryan, it's me Megan. I just wanted to say happy birthday and guess what? I'm moving back to the states to finish my last two years of med school! What do you think about that?"

Megan shook her head. 'No, that'd be too awkward. Besides, he's probably long since moved on. Time to stop living in the past, Meg...'

16 | The Third Wish

Somewhere in the states later that year…

"How in the world did you find out about this again?" Meg asked Edwin as she and her friends walked towards a small stadium.

"I have my ways," he smiled. "Besides," he continued. "I know that a certain quartet that's performing will certainly make your day. You can even say hi to lover boy. We'll be close enough to the front that there's no way he could miss you."

"I don't know about that," she smiled uncertainly.

"Come on, Meg," he said, drawing her close and hugging her as they walked. "Relax. We brought you here so you could have fun."

"Right… Fun…"

"Meg, I'm not going to lie to you and say that seeing you in some other guy's arms will make me happy. I still have feelings for you, you know. But if stepping aside to let you and your true love be together is what it takes to make you happy…" He shrugged. "If I can't make you happy, I may as well let you go to the one guy who can."

She smiled. "Thanks, Edwin. It means a lot knowing you're here to help me."

"Anything for you," he answered, giving her a kiss on the forehead.

"Hey guys, hurry up!" One of their friends called.

"I hear music. I don't want to miss any bit of this charity concert!"

Laughing, the two quickened their pace to catch up with the rest of the group.

An hour later, Meg found herself cheering her support as the latest performers took their bows and left the stage. "They were good," she said.

"Yeah. Not too bad," Edwin agreed.

"Who's next?" she asked, looking down to her program. She froze.

"Come on, don't worry," a friend on her right said, giving Meg a hug.

Edwin squeezed her hand as Pulse took the stage amid the screams.

Immediately, the foursome burst into one of their dance songs to pump up the already lively crowd. Megan couldn't help but smile as she watched the guys sing their hearts out. There was Josh, with his brown hair currently cut short in a crew cut and his tailored top doing little to hide the body he continued to work hard to keep in shape. Singing and dancing next to him was Matt, the musical master of the group, wearing a looser, more comfortable shirt. Third was Connor, the so-called baby of the group who was currently donning a classy tie and top that offset the boyish grin on his face. And on the far end of the stage was Ryan, blonde head currently mostly hidden by a black fedora he was wearing along with the shirt and light jacket he wore on stage. All the guys were wearing dark jeans and sneakers to tie the look together and frankly, Megan couldn't help but feel her heart ache seeing them all together again.

Edwin had been right though. Their group was close enough to the front and she was noticed. Without interrupting the song, she saw recognition cross Matt's face, and while Ryan introduced the next song, she noticed him whispering to Josh and Connor in the background. She could tell they wanted to let Ryan know of her presence, but she shook her head no, a pleading look on her face to not let him know just yet. That moment of hesitation was enough for them to miss the opportunity as the next song started.

Megan immediately recognized the first few words out of Matt's mouth and felt her throat and chest tighten. Sadness claimed her as the guys sang one of the ballads that had come out shortly after she and Ryan had stopped talking. She had to look away as she blinked back her tears.

As soon as the guys were done, Megan hurried to get up and leave. She felt Edwin squeeze her hand and tell her good luck, but she didn't understand why. All she knew was that she needed to get out now. Her emotions were getting the better of her and she desperately needed some fresh air to clear her mind. Once outside, she didn't rest until she got to where her friends had parked. Out in the parking lot, it was a lot quieter and she sat down on the trunk of Edwin's car, resting her head in her hands.

"You know, you're one hard lady to keep up with," a voice said next to her a few minutes later.

Startled, Meg looked up into a pair of brown eyes. "I'm sorry?"

"You're Megan, right?" he asked.

"Yeah. I'm sorry, do I know you?"

"We met once. I think it was on your birthday a couple years back."

"My birthday? I don't-"

"At that one theater. You were sitting next to Ryan. I asked to see your ticket."

Realization slowly dawned on her face. "Oh yeah. I remember now. Nice to meet you…"

"Reuben," he answered, shaking her offered hand.

"Right. Reuben. So what are you doing out here? Shouldn't you be helping watch over the guys or something?"

"Nah. I don't work for them anymore, not since they took their extended break. I just came to see how they were doing and to show my support."

"Oh, okay."

"What about you? When I saw you leave the audience, I thought you were on your way back to see the guys."

'Ahh, so that's probably what Edwin thought,' she thought to herself. "When did you see me?"

"I noticed the guys kept looking in that general direction and then saw you there."

A slight panicked look filled her face as she looked up to him. "Did they see me leave?"

"I can't say for sure. Why? Are you avoiding them?"

"No!" she said quickly. Then she lowered her head and sighed. "Maybe. I don't know."

"Megan, I'm sure they'd love to see you again."

"How can you say that? It's been so long, and Ryan and I ended on such bad terms…"

"Then why are you here?"

"My friends from med school bought tickets and begged for me to come along."

"And you came against your own will?"

"No. I came because I wanted to. I needed to check something."

"What was that?"

"I had to see how I felt about Ryan. It's one thing thinking on your own with only vague memories. It's another thing seeing him again in the flesh. No hiding there."

"And?" he asked gently.

"There's no denying it. I miss him terribly. All this time, I'd almost convinced myself that I was over him, that I was just kidding myself when I thought something could still be there. But one look at him brought back all the memories I'd hidden from myself. One look reminded me of how much I really do love the guy and how incomplete I really feel. I miss him so much but I can't do anything about it. This isn't some fairy tale where the princess just makes a wish and poof! Her deepest desires come true."

"Why? Does it have anything to do with the guy you were holding hands with in there?"

"Edwin? Certainly not." She shook her head to emphasize that point. "He and I are just friends. I have no romantic feelings for him."

"Then what's holding you back?"

She shrugged and sighed. "Just myself. I mean come on, Reuben. How do I tell Ryan that after all this time, I am still head over heels in love with him?"

He paused for a moment before answering. "I

think you just did."

"Huh? What are you talking ab…" She trailed off when she saw Reuben smile at her kindly before looking past her shoulders. "Oh…"

A heavy silence surrounded them in the parking lot as all waited for Megan to make the next move. "I think I've decided on my third wish then," she finally said slowly.

"And what's that?" Reuben asked gently.

She stalled for only a moment. "The only thing I can wish for now is to wish Ryan all the happiness in the world with everything he's got going for him."

"Is that really what you want," Ryan asked quietly as he closed the distance between himself and Megan.

"Yes," she answered, unable to look at him but fully aware of him looking hard at her.

"I don't think I can grant you that wish then, because I know of something I don't have right now that will make me even happier."

"What's that?"

He was standing right next to her and gently, he tucked a finger under her chin so he could look into her eyes. "It's you."

Neither noticed as Reuben discreetly left the couple to break the news to the rest of the guys. Ryan was too busy holding Meg in his arms, comforting her and letting her cry to release all the guilt she'd carried with her over the years. A couple of tears slipped down his cheek as well as he hugged her close, grateful to have her back in his arms.

17 | Happily Ever After Reprise

"I now pronounce you husband and wife," the minister announced. "You may kiss the bride."

Ryan felt like a weight had been lifted off his shoulders. All the anticipation, all the nervousness, all the worry, and now none of it mattered. He was now officially wed to the love of his life. Ryan turned to his left and beheld the vision of white before him. Smiling, he lifted up the thin veil that separated Megan's face from the world before dropping down his hands to grasp hers as he bent down to plant a sweet kiss onto her lips. Then he wrapped her in his arms, smiling as she slipped her own arms around his waist. "I love you so much," he breathed into her ear.

"I love you more," she replied, causing him to shake a little with laughter.

He pulled away a little bit to give her another quick kiss before taking her hand in his again to face their friends and families. Amid the cheering and clapping and congratulations, the couple slowly made their way out the door and into the sunlight. After their business at the church was done, the two went on ahead to the reception. Food and speeches aside, the two finally found some alone time as they danced their first dance together.

For a minute or so, they didn't talk, content to just be in each other's arms, her head tucked under his chin and their eyes closed. She pulled back a little though when she felt him chuckling to himself and looked up into his eyes. "What?"

He smiled and bent down so their foreheads touched. "It's official. You can't leave me anymore."

She smiled too. "As if I could ever leave you."

He shrugged a little. "You did once."

"And I came back. Two and some years on my own made me realize what a stupid mistake that was."

"You had to do what you had to do."

"Only you would forgive me so easily."

"You weren't the only one to learn something as a result of our little, unintended separation."

"Oh really? And what did you learn?"

He pulled back a little so he could stare straight into her eyes. "Losing you made me realize how incomplete my world was without you. You know, waking up that morning without you in my arms scared me more than I thought it would have, but then I saw that you were just at the desk and the world was all better again. But then to wake up every morning like that? All the success in the world, even having the love and support from my friends and family – it still felt like something was missing."

"I'm sorry," she began.

He interrupted her by shaking his head slightly. "Shh. Let me finish." He waited until she nodded her head before going on. He smiled, hugging her tight. "So yeah. Physically, I couldn't imagine anyone else in my arms. I like you. You fit," he teased and was rewarded with one of her amused smiles. He lifted one of his hands to her face, gently tracing her jawline with a thumb. Lightly, he outlined her lips with a finger, earning himself another smile. Her cheeks, slightly flushed from all the laughing and smiling she'd done all day, were soft to his touch. But her eyes were what captured him. He looked into those rich, dark brown eyes of hers and felt himself melt from the intensity of the love radiating from them. "You know, you're so beautiful."

"Oh please," she said, lowering her gaze, embarrassed.

He chuckled a little, drawing her face back up so he could see into her eyes again. "You stop that! Get used to it because you'll be hearing it for a long, long time. I can promise you that."

"You're going to spoil me."

"As your husband, I'm entitled to that privilege."

"As long as I'm the only who gets pampered."

"You're the only one who will ever have all my love, Meg. You're my match, physically and mentally." He smiled. "You know, you surprised me that night in the theater." She looked at him, curiosity plain in her eyes as she waited for him to go on. "Most other girls, once they realize who I am, act in either of two ways. One, they become a bubbling idiot, not knowing what to say or how to act... I could understand their shock, but it gets uncomfortable fast. Two, they immediately drape themselves all over me and show themselves off, treating me as if I were a trophy to be won. You surprised me because straight off the bat, you treated me just like any other normal guy, but what I've never told you, and what I'm a little embarrassed to admit now, is that you actually intimidated me a little."

"Me? Intimidate you?"

He nodded. "You know, I never told you, but I was already there when you came into the theater. I swear to you, every male head in that room turned around when you stepped in the door, myself included. And no joke, every female head turned to you with envy in their eyes. You were beautiful, carrying yourself with such grace and confidence; it was like the stage, the theater was yours. This was your territory. And then we noticed your friend and most of us turned away.

"When you tapped me on the shoulder to apologize, I was surprised that it was you. I hadn't noticed that it was you sitting next to me because I'd been so engrossed coordinating plans with Reuben and the guys for afterward. But then there was your apology and then the moment you knew who I was because I saw the recognition in your face. Yet you introduced me with my middle name to your friend and I didn't know how to take that. For one, I was grateful. For another, I was wondering what you wanted in return."

Megan's eyes opened wide with shock. "I would never-"

"I know, Meg," he interrupted her again. "I know that now because I know you better, but you understand my precaution, especially when you asked something of me, asking if I could see you again that week. You're a force to be reckoned with, you know."

"So people tell me," she laughed.

"And it's the truth. Jumping ahead, you scared me when you left that morning. You were so angry, and I really did not like bearing the brunt of that emotional outburst. But as time passed, I realized it was exactly that passion that had me drawn to you before. You always give it your all, Meg, whether you're concerned with school or clinic or your family and friends. I'm a very lucky man to have such a beautiful, intelligent, strong woman as my wife."

"Intelligent, I'll give you. Beautiful, maybe. That's more your call than mine. But strong?" She smiled a little. "Ryan, you didn't see what a complete wreck I was without you by my side. When I heard that you'd already gone to the airport and left that day…" She shook her head, trying to banish the memory from her mind. "I couldn't blame you. It was all my fault for being so stupid as to ever think you didn't support me. It was a shock to you, but I let emotion overrule any rational thought in my head. I called, but that wasn't enough. I wanted to see you and tell you how sorry I was so much, but at the same time, I was so scared you'd be angry with me, that you'd turn me away just like I'd done to you, and I wouldn't have blamed you for that either. I hated myself so much so that it affected my work, and it wasn't until I realized that finals were on top of me that I pulled myself together, and even then, only just barely.

"Once those were over, I just broke down. I couldn't do anything. Ben and Lori and everyone else can attest to that. Dr. Keen even forced me to take a vacation because my mind just wasn't where it needed to be.

"And then it was time for me to leave. I didn't want to go, knowing things weren't complete between us, but I was still too afraid to do anything about it. So I wrote the letter as a last ditch effort, but I knew it wasn't enough for either you or me."

She nodded when he acknowledged the letter, and then she reached up a hand to wipe away the tear that had spilled as he listened to her. "See? It still brings us a lot of hurt and pain bringing it up. I was so insecure then. I wanted you back, but I knew I was being selfish there. Still, one of the things that kept me going was the hope that one day, I'd be able to face you and somehow make it all better." She stared up into his eyes. "You know, I'm not always the confident one. I was scared of you when I realized who you were. I was scared of what you thought of me. I wondered why you let me get close. And then I wondered if you'd ever take me back."

"Meg, you couldn't keep me away," he smiled, kissing her softly to ease away her fears.

After breaking apart, she sighed happily. "You know I love you, right?"

"If I didn't, I wouldn't have asked you to marry me," he teased, smiling down at her.

She laughed. "Well in that case, then I guess I should be thankful that you chose to keep me, huh?"

"I didn't do anything more than ask. You were the one to accept the proposal, you know."

She grinned. "That's true. You won't make me regret that choice, will you?"

"Never," he promised. "I love you, Meg, and I

always will."

"Good," she smiled. "Here's to forever then," she said as she lowered his head for another sweet kiss.

IN GRATITUDE

Thank you, AB, for helping me brainstorm lyrics. And thank you, dear reader, for taking your time to read through my next attempt at fiction. I would greatly appreciate it if you took a moment to leave an honest review on Amazon and share with others via social media:

https://www.amazon.com/-/e/B078M9S7S1

ABOUT THE AUTHOR

M. A. VALDELLON is a dreamer at heart.

When she's not immersed in the literary world, she can often be found playing and creating with crystals and music, cuddling with her furry loved ones, enjoying hot chocolate, and mentoring students and patients on their eyes and health in the Bay Area, California.

With two books already published and at least two more on the way, M. A. is certainly keeping herself out of trouble, but is not too busy as to be unavailable. You can contact her by email directly on her website, http://melissavaldellon.com/, and she will personally get back to you shortly.

Her next fiction, *Even In War*, will be released April 2018.